"I Just Wanted Us Both To Be Clear About What Was Going On," Camille Said.

"Damn good sex is what went on," Pete replied. "The best sex I can remember. Chemistry was over the top. If you feel differently or are trying to tell me that you regret it—"

"I don't regret it."

"If you want something more from me…"

"I don't want a damn thing, you blockheaded dolt! And there's nothing wrong with 'just sex,' either! Everything doesn't have to end up in a compli__ heavy relationship, for heaven's sake!"

"So what's the problem?"

"There is no problem! And d__ whipped around and stomped __ the damn man and where did it __ want to be cared about. Well, fine__

She didn't want him to care about h__, either.

She walked so fast that she got a stitch in her side—except that somehow, that stitch seemed to be located right over her heart….

Dear Reader,

Thank you for choosing Silhouette Desire—where passion is guaranteed in every read. Things sure are heating up with our continuing series DYNASTIES: THE BARONES. Eileen Wilks's *With Private Eyes* is a powerful romance that helps set the stage for the daring conclusion next month. And if it's more continuing stories that you want— we have them. TEXAS CATTLEMAN'S CLUB: THE STOLEN BABY launches this month with Sara Orwig's *Entangled with a Texan.*

The wonderful Peggy Moreland is on hand to dish up her share of Texas humor and heat with *Baby, You're Mine,* the next installment of her TANNERS OF TEXAS series. Be sure to catch Peggy's Silhouette Single Title, *Tanner's Millions,* on sale January 2004. Award-winning author Jennifer Greene marks her much-anticipated return to Silhouette Desire with *Wild in the Field,* the first book in her series THE SCENT OF LAVENDER.

Also for your enjoyment this month, we offer Katherine Garbera's second book in the KING OF HEARTS series. *Cinderella's Christmas Affair* is a fabulous "it could happen to you" plot guaranteed to leave her fans extremely satisfied. And rounding out our selection of delectable stories is *Awakening Beauty* by Amy J. Fetzer, a steamy, sensational tale.

More passion to you!

Melissa Jeglinski

Melissa Jeglinski
Senior Editor, Silhouette Desire

Please address questions and book requests to:
Silhouette Reader Service
U.S.: 3010 Walden Ave., P.O. Box 1325, Buffalo, NY 14269
Canadian: P.O. Box 609, Fort Erie, Ont. L2A 5X3

JENNIFER GREENE

Wild *in the* Field

Silhouette® Desire®

Published by Silhouette Books

America's Publisher of Contemporary Romance

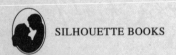

SILHOUETTE BOOKS

ISBN 0-373-76545-2

WILD IN THE FIELD

Visit Silhouette at www.eHarlequin.com

Printed in U.S.A.

JENNIFER GREENE

lives near Lake Michigan with her husband and two children. Before writing full-time, she worked as a teacher and a personnel manager.

Ms. Greene has written more than fifty category romances, for which she has won numerous awards, including three RITA® Awards from the Romance Writers of America in the Best Short Contemporary Books category, and she entered RWA's Hall of Fame in 1998.

To Lar—
For letting me rescue even the impossibly ugly dogs, cats
and critters over the years.
Don't worry, love.
I'll never tell anyone what a softie you are.

One

Once a month, Pete MacDougal braced for a full-scale rebellion. And once every month, he got it.

Only the nature of the weapons and attacks varied. The look on the faces of his fourteen-year-old sons was always the same: A never-give-in-determination in the eyes, an unrelenting stubbornness in the chins, a cocky attitude written on their every feature.

It was bad enough to have two teenagers in the house, worse yet to have twins, but the real insult was that the kids took after him. It just wasn't fair.

"Look, Dad. You just don't get it. You're missing the point of living without women. We're supposed to be *free*."

"Uh-huh," Pete said, and from his key position in the front hall, slapped a mop and bucket in Simon's hands. His sidekick—and Sean was the absolute spit-

ting image of his brother except for one errant cowlick—
was trying to slowly back away from the vacuum.

"Come on, Dad. Remember about *free?* We're supposed to be free to be ourselves. Free to not eat vegetables. Free to not do dishes until we run out. Free to
wear our boots in the house. Free to live how we
want."

The vacuum nozzle was slapped into Sean's hand—
but Simon elbowed in front of him. "You always said
we should think for ourselves, remember, Dad? Well,
we finally got a day off from school because of the
blizzard, so I think the last thing we should be doing
is *cleaning.*"

Sean accidentally let the vacuum nozzle drop. "And,
like, what's the point, you know? As soon as you clean,
the dirt comes right back. What's wrong with dirt anyway? I like dirt. Simon likes dirt. Gramps likes dirt.
You're the only one—"

"Dirt keeps the women away, right, Dad? Like an
apple keeps the doctor awa—"

"Enough. I've had it with the lip." Pete knew he'd
lose his temper. He always did. The only question
every month was when. "I don't want to hear another
word. Unless you both want to be grounded for the rest
of your lives, the floors are getting washed and the
carpets vacuumed. And the bathrooms—hell, the health
department wouldn't go near your bathroom upstairs.
It stinks. Now move it—"

"I'm not doing the bathroom," Sean told his
brother.

"Well, I'm sure not—"

Pete's voice raised. "BOTH bathrooms upstairs.
And I want all towels and dirty clothes down the
chute—" He saw the bucket crash down on Simon's

head, followed by the mop cracking over Sean's. Yowls followed—both of them sounded like tomcats auditioning for a back alley fight. The yowls inspired more blows, followed by desperate claims of pain, followed by pokes and giggles and more desperate claims of pain.

"NOTHING is going to get you out of chores, do you hear me? And I don't care if it takes until midnight—this house is getting cleaned up. If I have to knock your heads together—"

Both kids knew damn well he never had and never would knock their heads together, but usually the threat got their attention. It didn't work this afternoon. The senior MacDougal unfortunately chose that moment to poke his head over the banister. Ian leaned heavily on his cane and looked more frail by the week, but he offered full-bellowed support to the boys on the benefit of dirt and the joys of life without women. Ian MacDougal was inarguably the most worthless grandfather this side of Poughkeepsie. Worthless...but popular. The boys immediately begged their grandfather to take their side against their slave-driving, cruel, unfair, uncaring, unreasonable father.

"I'm so sick of hearing this malarkey every month that I could punch a wall. The place is a sty. There is NO argument, and that goes for you, too, Dad. Now, all of you, GET TO IT."

Well, they finally budged, but whether the old farmhouse would end up destroyed or cleaned, Pete wasn't sure. The boys clattered upstairs, dragging tools and utensils to make the maximum possible racket. The minute they were out of sight, a series of dramatic noises followed. The source of the noises wasn't clear, but seemed a possible cross between trumpeting ele-

phants, screaming banshees, bloodthirsty soldiers and
whining brothers. A stereo blared on, followed by a
television—both played at volumes that could be heard
over a vacuum cleaner. Or a sonic boom, Pete mused.

He almost missed the sound of the doorbell—actually, he almost didn't recognize it. No one used a doorbell in White Hills, Vermont—at least not at the
MacDougal house. Particularly on a snow-stormy day
in March when even the sturdiest New England farmer
was holed up inside.

When he yanked open the front door, fistfuls of snow
were hurled in his face, which didn't shock him half
as much as his visitor.

"Pete? I need to ask you a favor."

"Well, sure. Come on in." The Campbells had the
neighboring property—in fact, the Campbells and the
MacDougals had probably come over on the same ship
from Scotland a million generations before. Long before the American Revolution, for damn sure. The
MacDougals tended to raise sons, where the Campbells
favored having daughters. Pete had grown up with
three Campbell sisters himself, had gone to school with
Violet.

"Hey, Dad! Who's at the do—?" Sean started to
scream down the stairs, galloped halfway, then saw
who was standing in the doorway. "Hey, Ms. Campbell," he said at a lower decibel level.

"Hey, Sean."

Sean disappeared. The vacuum died. The stereo died.
The TV died. All signs of life silenced. They were all
afraid of Violet Campbell. Violet was… Well, Pete
wasn't sure how to explain Violet to his kids. She'd
always seemed normal in high school, but a few years
ago, she'd come back home after a divorce with the

brains of a poodle. Like now, on a day colder than a witch's heart, she wore her blond hair flowing down her back, flighty boots, earrings almost too big to make it through the doorway and a pretty purple coat that couldn't keep a goose warm. She was about one hundred pounds of froufrou, and on sight threw Pete's all-male household into a panic attack.

Except for Pete. How could you be scared of somebody you'd gone to school with? It'd be like rejecting a sister. Whether she was weird or not was irrelevant. Automatically he ushered her inside and closed the door, facing her with resigned patience. "Take off your coat. You want coffee? By this time of day it's thicker than mud, but it'll still be hot—" The instant he caught a straight look at her face, he changed gears. "What's wrong?"

"Thanks, but I don't need coffee. I won't stay long." She pulled off her gloves, obviously on edge, revealing four rings on each hand. Immediately, her hands began fluttering, as restless as a trapped canary. "What's wrong is my sister, Pete. Camille. I need to drive down to Boston for a few days."

One minute Pete was fine. The next he felt as if someone had slugged him in the stomach. Just hearing Camille's name could do that. Violet may have been like an honorary sister to him, but Camille sure wasn't. "Hell. Everybody said Cam was finally doing okay. Is she sick? Hurt? What can I do?"

Violet shook her head. "I only wish you *could* do something. I'm about beside myself. And I'm scared to drive in this icy weather, but I have to go there. Get her to come home. It may take me a couple of days or more. I don't know. But the thing is, I'm leaving my business, the greenhouses, my cats—"

"Forget it. I'll take care of that stuff."

"The greenhouse temperature has to be—"

"Violet, I've done it for you before. I know what to do, what to watch for." He was annoyed she felt she had to ask. MacDougals had been taking care of Campbells for years and vice versa. That's how it was in White Hills. After everyone finished fighting over sex, religion and politics, they still took care of their neighbors. And Pete knew perfectly well how temperamental her greenhouses were to caretake, so he sure as hell didn't want to waste time talking about it. "What happened? I thought Camille was finally on the mend. I mean, obviously, she had a hell of a time. But it's been months since whozit died—"

Violet unbuttoned the top of her jacket, took a long breath. "I know. We all thought that was the rough part. Her losing Robert like that. Barely married a year, so much in love, and then to lose everything in a stupid street robbery." Violet's eyes welled up. "She loved him so much."

"Yeah. I heard." Pete saw the tears, and figured he'd better do something quick and drastic before she started *really* crying on him. But a burst of mental pictures flashed through his mind, ransoming his attention and his heartbeat both. All he could think about was Camille.

Cam was four years younger than him—which meant, when they were in school, that he'd have been way out of line to look at her in a personal way. But he remembered her wedding. She hadn't been too young then. She'd looked like God's gift to a sexy wedding night—deeply in love with her groom—full of laughter and light, full of secret smiles and sexual promises, her face glowing and her gorgeous dark eyes softened with love.

Pete had always had a soft spot for her. All right, he admitted it—more than a soft spot. He'd had a dug-in, could-never-shake pull for her. But those feelings had made him feel forbidden and guilty, initially because she'd been too young, and then later because a good man just didn't think about the bride of another guy that way. Still, when he'd heard about the couple getting attacked by thugs last year, he remembered feeling profound relief she hadn't been the one killed.

"The neighbors all said she was finally recovered," he pressed Violet again.

"And that was a miracle in itself. The physical recovery took months as it was. She was in the hospital for ages. Her beautiful face—she was so battered up, her face, her ribs, the broken leg—"

"But that's the point. Everyone said she was finally on her feet again—so what happened? Has there been some kind of setback? What?" God, getting Violet to the point was like motivating a mule to win a horse race.

Violet threw up her hands, did more of that fluttering thing. "It's complicated. Camille always calls home a couple of times a week. Only suddenly she quit calling. And when I tried to track her down, I found out that her phone's been disconnected. So then I got in touch with her apartment neighbor. Twilla something. This Twilla says Camille lost her job, hasn't been out of the apartment in two weeks or more. Mail's piled up, newspapers, trash. She says she knocked on Camille's door, thinking she had to be sick or something, but Cam was in there and nearly snapped her head off."

"Say what?" Camille had always been one of those

joyful, happy-go-lucky people. No temper, no temperament. She'd never had a moody bone in her entire body.

Violet hugged her arms. "I don't know what to think. But Twilla said she's turned totally mean."

"That's ridiculous. Camille couldn't be mean in a million years. It's not in her."

"It didn't used to be. I think it's about the trial, Pete. The trial of those three thugs."

Pete frowned. "You mean, the guys who robbed her? The boys and I were gone for spring break when the trial ended, but I thought they were all found guilty."

"They were. Only the guilty verdict wasn't worth much. The one who actually killed Robert only got seven years—and he can get out after three for good behavior. The other two got even lighter sentences. They could be back on the streets in less than two years."

"WHAT? They kill whozits and almost beat Camille to death, and a few years in prison is the only penalty they got?"

Violet's eyes welled again. "That's all. The judge seemed to think there were extenuating circumstances. They'd had no record before, and even though they'd all chosen to get high, they had no way to know the drug had been laced with some extra chemicals. They were all in this induced psychotic state, according to the testimony. So the judge didn't seem to think they were totally to blame. Anyway, apparently the sentence came down about a month ago. It was a long trial, and God knows I'd been following it—so was everyone in the family. And Camille called when the sentence came down, but that was it. She was upset, we knew that.

But that was the last time she contacted anyone, as far as I know." Violet grabbed her gloves, obviously too agitated to stand still and talk any longer.

"Bring her home, damn it," Pete said.

"That's what I'm going to do. Drive there, pack up her stuff, bring her home."

"If she won't come, you call me. I'll drive there and help."

"According to her neighbor, I'll be lucky if she lets *me* in. But I figure I can always ask Daisy if I really need help."

Pete didn't follow. "Isn't your other sister still living in France?"

"Yeah, but she'd fly over in two seconds if I called. She flew home when Camille was first attacked and in the hospital. So did Mom and Dad, of course. But for this problem—I just want to see what's what for myself before I call in the cavalry." Violet opened the front door. More fistfuls of snow howled in, but she turned back to him, appearing not to notice. "Daisy is kind of like the calvary. She's just a take-charge, bossy kind of person—"

Pete knew Daisy. He also knew that once Violet got chatty, she was hard to shut down, so he tried to get her back on track. She gave him keys to the house and greenhouse, then proceeded to flibber and flabber on about security and temperatures and the fragility of her lavender strains and the cat and the trickiness of the furnace if the temperature dropped below zero and how the back door stuck.

By the time she left, an inch of snow had accumulated in the front hall. He closed the door and watched out the side window as Violet backed her flower-decaled van out of the driveway, bouncing through snowdrifts, not looking in either direction. He wasn't sure if either the driveway or the mailbox was going to survive her driving—but truthfully, his mind wasn't really on the middle Campbell sister, but the baby in the family.

He scraped a hand through his hair, wishing he'd asked Violet a dozen more questions…yet knowing he couldn't. Just because he'd always had a private hard case for Camille didn't mean he had any right to know—or right to interfere either. Further, his skill and effectiveness with women was measured by his ex-wife—who'd effectively ripped him off for everything but the kitchen sink…and his sons.

God knew, his sons were full time—sometimes a full-time nightmare and sometimes a full-time job. But either way, he had no time to dwell on the worrisome picture Violet had painted in his mind. Camille couldn't be his problem. It was just upsetting, that was all. To picture anyone as joyful and full of spirit as Cam, brought down by so much tragedy so young. Camille always had a heart bigger than Vermont, more love than an ocean, more laughter than could fill a whole sky.

It made him sick to think about her hurting.

"Pssst. Dad." The daredevil hanging over the second story railing was, of course, risking life and limb. "Ms. Campbell—is she gone? Is it safe to come down?"

"Yeah, she's gone."

In another moment, his son's spitting image hung over the railing, too. "Are you sick or something? What's the matter with you, Dad? You're not yelling at us."

"I will," Pete promised them absently, but when he

didn't immediately come through with a good, solid respectable bellow, the boys seemed to panic.

"We're not cleaning," Sean announced.

"Yeah, we're going on strike," Simon said. "Gramps is going on strike with us. So it's three against one."

Maybe he'd failed a wife, but he'd never fail his boys. Since they were expecting him to scream and yell, he forced his mind off Camille and thumped up the stairs to deliver the lecture they wanted.

Two

When Camille heard the knock on the door, her heart slammed in instant panic—but that was just a stupid, knee-jerk response from the attack. She'd been home and forcefully installed in the cottage by Violet for three weeks now. She was safe. She *knew* she was safe. But somehow, even all these months after the attack, sudden noises and shadows still made her stomach jump clear to her throat.

Someone knocked on the door again—which she purposefully ignored. She just as easily ignored the pounding after that. But then came her sister's insistent voice calling, "Yoo-hoo! Camille? CAMILLE?"

Camille didn't budge from old, horsehair rocker in the far corner of the living room, but hearing Vi whining her name reminded her of how much she'd always disliked it. Mom had named all three daughters after flowers, so she could have gotten Violet or Daisy, but no, she had to get Camille. Practically by definition people seemed to assume that a Camille was a dark-haired, dark-eyed, sultry romantic. The dark hair and dark eyes were true, but the rest of the image was completely off.

These last months, she'd turned mean. Not just a little mean, but horned-toad mean. Porcupine-mean. Curmudgeon-rude and didn't-give-a-damn-about-anyone mean.

"All right, Cam, honey." When no one answered, Violet's voice turned so patient that Camille wanted to open the door just to smack her one. "I'll leave lunch on the table at noon, but I want you up at the house for dinner. You don't have to talk. You don't have to do anything. But unless you're up there at six—and I actually see you eat something—I'm calling Mom and Daisy both."

Camille's eyes creaked open in the dim room. Something stirred in her stomach. A touch of an ordinary emotion…like worry. Not that she gave a hoot—about anything or anyone. But the threat of having both her mother and oldest sister sicced on her made Cam break out in a cold sweat. The Campbell women, allied together, could probably make a *stone* sweat. She just wasn't up to battling with them.

With a resigned sigh, she pushed herself out of the old, horsehair rocker to search for a drink.

Rain drooled down the dirty windows, making it hard to see without a light, but she didn't turn one on. The past weeks had passed in a blur. She remembered Violet barging into the apartment in Boston, finding her curled up in bed, shaking her, scolding her, packing her up. She remembered driving to Vermont in a blizzard. She remembered refusing to live in the warm, sturdy farmhouse where they'd grown up, fighting with Violet over whether the old cottage on the place was even livable.

It wasn't. But then Camille wasn't livable either, so the place had worked for her fine.

She stumbled around now, stalking around suitcases and boxes. She hadn't unpacked anything from Boston. No reason to. She didn't want anything. But eventually she located the flat briefcase on the scarred oak bureau. She clicked the locks, pulled it open. Once upon a time, the briefcase had been filled with colorful files and advertising projects and marketing studies. Now it held a complete array of airline-sized liquor bottles.

Quite a few were missing, although not as many as she'd planned. She hadn't given up her goal of becoming an alcoholic, but the ambition was a lot tougher to realize than she ever expected. Frowning, she filched and fingered through the collection. Crème de cocoa was out of the question—she was never trying that ghastly stuff again. Ditto for the vodka. And the scotch. And the gin.

Squinting, she discovered a bitsy bottle of Kahlúa. She wrestled with the lid, finally successfully unscrewed it, guzzled in a gulp, swallowed, and then opened her mouth to let out the fumes.

Holy moly. Her eyes teared and her throat surely scarred over from the burn.

As hard as she was trying to destroy her life with liquor, it just wasn't working well. She set down the mini-bottle—she was going to finish it!—she only needed to take a few minutes to renew her determination.

She sank down in the creaky rocker again, closing

her eyes. Maybe the drinking wasn't going so well, but other things were.

Several weeks ago, she'd mistakenly believed that she wanted to die. Since then, she'd realized that one part of her was alive—totally alive, consumingly alive.

The rage.

All around her was the evidence. Violet had tried to give her a phone, but she'd trashed it. The cottage behind the barns had been built for a great grandmother who'd wanted to live independently, so there was no totally destroying the charm. There was just a front room, bedroom and kitchen, but the casement windows bowed, and the bedroom had a slanted ceiling, and the living room had a huge limestone fireplace with a sit-down hearth. She hadn't fixed any of it. Hadn't looked at any of it either. She'd been sleeping on a hard mattress with a bald pillow and no bedding. Cobwebs filled the corners; the floors hadn't been swept, and the cupboards were empty.

She couldn't remember the last time she brushed her hair or changed clothes.

Eventually this had to stop. She realized that in an intellectual way, but emotionally, there only seemed one thing inside of her. All she wanted was to sit all day and seep with the rage, steep with it, sleep with it. Fester it. Ache with it. My God. It had been bad enough to lose Robert. Bad enough to wake up in a hospital bed with a face so battered she couldn't recognize herself, bruises and breaks that made her cry to touch, lips too swollen to talk…and that was before she'd been told Robert was dead.

Initially, the grief had ripped through her like a cyclone that wouldn't quit. It just wrenched and tore and never let up. But then came the trial. She'd been so

positive that the trial would at least bring her the relief
and satisfaction of justice. Every time she closed her
eyes, she saw the dark street, heard her laughing with
Robert, complaining about walking in high heels from
the party on the balmy fall night, and then there they
were. The bastards, the drug-high bastards. There was
no *reason* for them to start punching her, playing her,
scaring her. They'd have given them all their money
in a blink. But it wasn't money they wanted. Robert—
he'd tried to protect her, tried to get in front of her.
That's why they were meaner to him. Why he ended
up dead.

All three of them had looked clean-cut and young in
court—because they were. They had cried their eyes
out, which had impressed the judge, too. They'd come
from good families, had no records, weren't even drug
users—they just made one mistake, thought they'd ex-
periment one time, and foolishly bought some mixed
cocktail that caused psychotic behavior. It was a tragic
accident, their attorney claimed. The boys weren't
hardened criminals, nothing like that. And the judge
had given them the most lenient sentences possible.

That's when the rage was born. Camille remembered
the day in court, feeling the slow, huge, hot well of
disbelief. A few years in jail and they'd be out. Easy
for them. They hadn't lost their soul mate. They hadn't
lost anything but a few years, where she'd lost everything. Her life had been completely, irreversibly, hopelessly destroyed.

She stared blankly at the cracks in the stucco ceiling,
hearing the drizzle of rain. Inside of her there was nothing but a hollow howl. It wasn't getting any better. She
couldn't seem to think past the red-sick haze of rage.
She'd tried curling up for days. She'd tried not eating.

She'd tried hurling things and breaking things. She'd tried silence. She'd tried—and was still trying—drinking.

No matter what she tried, though, she couldn't seem to make it pass. She couldn't go under, around, through it. The rage was just there.

At some point, she got up and finished the shot of Kahlúa.

And at some point after that, she jerked out of the rocker and chased fast for the bathroom. The Kahlúa was as worthless as all the other darn liquors. It refused to stay down.

By the time she finished hurling, she was extra mean. She stood in the bathroom doorway, sweat beading on her brow, weakness aching in every muscle in her damn body. She wasn't sure she was strong enough to lift a dust ball. Her throat felt as it had been knifed open and her stomach as if she'd swallowed hot steel wool.

With her luck, she was going to end up the first wanna-be alcoholic in history with an allergy to alcohol. Either that, or Kahlúa had joined the long list of liquors her body seemed to reject.

Thinking that possibly she could nap—and maybe even sleep this time—she turned toward the bedroom…just as she heard another knock on the door.

"Aw, come on, Violet. I'll come up to the house for dinner. But right now, just leave me alone."

"It's not Violet. It's me. Your neighbor. Pete MacDougal."

A charge volted through her pulse as if she'd touched a volatile electric cord. Pete didn't have to identify himself for her to recognize his voice. There was a time that voice would have comforted her. Pete's clipped tenor was part of her childhood, as familiar as the rail fence and the tree house in the big maple and the toboggan hill between the MacDougals and Campbells.

She'd never played with Pete because he was older, Violet's age. But she'd toddled after him for years with puppy eyes. When he was around, he'd lift her over the fence so she wouldn't have to walk around, and he'd pulled her sled back up the hill, and he'd let her invade the sacred tree house when all the other kids said she was still a baby.

Pete was not just her childhood hero; he'd been an extra zesty spice to her blood because the four year age difference made him forbidden. Further, he was ultracool, with his biker shoulders and thick dark hair and smoky eyes. He was the oldest of three brothers, where she was the youngest of three sisters, which she'd always felt gave them a key connection. What that connection was, she'd never pinned down exactly. She'd just wanted to have something in common with Pete MacDougal. Coming from three-children families and living in Vermont had seemed enough to be critical bonding factors when she was a kid.

Those memories were all sweet and a little embarrassing and definitely fun—but not now. Right *now*, she didn't want to see anyone she'd once cared about, and Pete's voice, specifically, hurt like a sting. He had one of those full-of-life, uniquely male voices—full of sex and testosterone and energy and virility.

It wasn't Robert's voice. In fact, it was nothing at all like Robert's sweet voice. But that bolt of vibrant masculine tenor reminded her of everything she'd lost. And because she felt stung, she stung back.

"Go the hell away."

He knocked again, as if he hadn't heard her. "Could you just open the door for a minute?"

"NO."

He knocked again.

What did it take? A sledgehammer? "Damn it, Pete. I don't want visitors. I don't need sympathy. I don't want help. I don't want to talk to anyone. I just want to be left alone. GO AWAY."

When he knocked the fourth time, she yanked open the door from sheer exasperation. If the only way to get rid of him was to punch him in the nose, then she was about to slug him good—and never mind that he was almost a foot taller than her.

Instantly she noticed that foot-taller. Noticed his black-and-white wool shirt, his oak height, the hint of wet mahogany in his damp hair, that his good-looking sharp-boned face still had smoky, sexy eyes. She also noticed that he wedged a size-thirteen boot in the door before she could slam it on him again.

In that same blast of a second, he looked her over, too—but he didn't make out as if he noticed that she was in days-old clothes, her hair unkempt, her face paler than a mime's. He didn't make out as if he noticed anything personal about her at all. He just said, "I have to tell you something about your sister."

"So tell me and get out."

"Hey, I'm trying." He didn't force his way in, just kept that big boot wedged in the doorway. He leaned his shoulder in the jamb, which insured he had a view of the inside. But if he saw the piles of boxes and packing debris in the dreary light, he made no comment. "It's Violet. I don't know what on earth's wrong with your sister. But something sure is."

"I've seen her very day. She's perfectly fine."

"Ditsy as always," Pete concurred. "But after she came home after the divorce, she started playing in the greenhouse. By last spring, she'd added another greenhouse and opened her herb business. Then last spring, she laid off Filbert Green—you know, the man your dad hired after he retired, to take care of the land—"

"What's any of this to you, Pete?" Rain hissed in the yard, splashed off the eaves. The chill was starting to seep in the cottage, but he didn't seem to care. He seemed intent on just blocking her doorway for an indefinite period of time.

"It's nothing to me. But it is to you. Have you looked around the farm since you got home?"

"No. Why would I? I've got nothing to do with the farm. Violet can do whatever she wants to." The darn man never moved his eyes, never showed the slightest reaction, but she kept having the sense he was taking in everything about her.

"Camille—you remember how your mother always grew a patch of lavender? You Campbell women always loved the stuff—"

"For heaven's sake, Pete. Get to the point."

"Your sister's been breeding all kinds of lavender."

"So what?"

He sighed, rubbed his chin. "You want me to get to the point, but it isn't that easy. She's gone hog-wild in the greenhouses. Take a look out your window, walk around, you'll see. She has to have better than twenty acres of lavender planted."

"That's ridiculous," Camille announced.

He didn't argue with her. He just said, "I think the Herb Haven store is doing okay for her. Pulls in more kooks and New Agers than I can believe. But even if she didn't have her hands full with the retail and the greenhouses, Violet doesn't know about land, never did, never cared. And that's fine, but it's one thing to let a field go wild, and another to let twenty acres of lavender get out of control—and I'm talking completely out of control. She's in trouble, Camille.''

''My sister is not in trouble with anything,'' Camille told him firmly.

''Okay. I didn't come to argue. In fact, I told you everything I came to say.'' He not only stepped back, but closed the door for her, firmly and quietly. She heard the thud of his boot step on the porch, then nothing as he strode toward his white pickup.

She watched him from the grimy window—even though she didn't mean to look. Neither Pete Mac-Dougal nor his opinions were any of her business. God knew what that visit was all about, but it didn't matter.

Violet wasn't in trouble. Cam had seen her every damn day. Vi was dressing like a model for a gypsy catalog with all the sweeping scarves and flowing blond hair and all—but Violet had always been a girly-girl. She never had a tomboy bone in her body, probably came out of the womb asking Mom for a credit card and directions to the mall. The point being, she might be going a little overboard with the froufrou thing, but Violet was still Violet.

Camille stood in the doorway a moment longer, and then with a sinking feeling of defeat and exhaustion, padded toward the bedroom.

When it came down to it, even if Violet were in trouble—which she wasn't—Camille likely couldn't muster enough energy to help her anyway. Right now she couldn't even help herself. For a brief moment,

Pete had sparked something vibrant and unexpected...
but that was just a fluke.

There was just nothing in her anymore. Nothing.

It was still raining four days later. The theory about
April showers bringing May flowers was all well and
good, but these April rains were bleakly chill and relentless—which was why Camille spent two hours hiking outside. The weather suited her mood perfectly.

She didn't care what Pete MacDougal had told her—
in any way. She hadn't given him another thought—in
any way.

The fresh rain stung her cheeks, but still she tromped
the fields until her legs ached and she was cold and
damp from the inside out. By the time she clomped
into her sister's kitchen, it was just after six. In the
back hall, she shed field boots, her father's thrown-out
barn jacket and an old cap. They had given her little
protection against the weather. Her dark hair was strag-
gling-wet at the edges, her jeans hemmed with ice-cold
mud, and she couldn't stop shivering.

Naturally, her sister caught her before she had time
to run some hot water on her hands.

"Sheesh, Camille. You're going to catch your death.
Come in and get yourself warm, you goose." Violet
had always been a bully. She hustled her into the
kitchen, where warm yellow light pooled on the old
glass cabinets and potbellied stove and round oak table.
Pots simmered on the stove. Counters were crowded
with dishes. Smells choked the air.

Dinner was going to be another petrifying meal,
Camille sensed.

It was. She pried open lids and covers. The main
course appeared to be cod stuffed with spinach. The
salad looked to be a bunch of pungent herbs that
smelled as if they could not only get a body's system

moving—but moving permanently. The drink was some herbal concoction in a pitcher. Violet hadn't served normal food since Camille could remember.

"We're going to start with some Fish Soup Normandy tonight. We've got to build you up, Cam. You're not just skinnier than a rail, those jeans are about to fall off. For Pete's sake, I'm not sure you could find your butt with a magnifying glass. I'm not sure you even have one anymore."

Camille cut to more important issues. "What's in the Normandy soup?"

"Oh, this and that. Celery, onions, carrot, lemon. Herbs and seasonings. And fish heads, of course—"

Camille muttered a swearword. The bad one. Violet just smiled as she scurried around the kitchen. Tonight she was wearing a paisley blouse of some flowing material, her pale blond hair braided with a scarf. "I've been working up a storm in the greenhouses. I know it's hard to believe, but it's going to be warm in just a couple more weeks...." She glanced up and said carefully, "I saw you out walking."

Camille scooped up silverware and plates to set the table.

"That's the first I've seen you come out of the cottage—except for coming up here for meals, obviously. You were starting to scare me, Cam."

"Nothing to be scared about." She took a breath. "And I'm not going to mooch off you forever. I know I'm not bringing in any money. I don't want to be a burden. I just—"

"You're no burden and you're not mooching, you dimwit. The farm's yours no different than it's mine and Daisy's. You can live here forever, if you want. In fact, there's tons of space here at the house, you know that—"

"No." There was no way she could stay here. Her Campbell ancestors had sailed here from Scotland, homesteaded here, put down the first layer of brick and stone. Although generations had added on, it remained a sturdy, serious house with white trim and a shake roof. Inside, the plank floors were polished to a shine. There was still a cane rocker and rag rug by the kitchen potbellied stove. Violet had added the chintz upholstery, the frilly curtains, the Live Well-Love Much-Laugh Often type of homey slogans. Cats nested on most surfaces. The kitchen that had been blue and white, was now red and white, with pots of herbs clustered in the sink window.

And just like when they were growing up, Violet was still incessantly chattering. "Mom and Dad called…"

Camille immediately tensed.

"But I told them you were doing fine."

There. She relaxed again.

"But then Daisy called. I told her the same thing, that you were doing fine. But you know Daisy. She started talking in that new French accent of hers, bristled up, and said if you don't call her within the next few days, she's flying home. I think she actually might, Cam. She needs to hear from you herself."

"Well, she's not going to." Violet might boss her around at times, but she was pretty much a live-and-let-live kind of sister. Daisy was a nightmare. "Just keep telling her I'm fine."

"Okay."

Camille stuck a fork in the cod, pushed it around her plate. "Behind the barn, all those acres on the east

slope, where everything used to freeze out for Dad...
what are you doing there, Vi? With all that lavender?''

Violet brightened. ''Camille! You asked me a question! You realize, this is the first conversation you've
actually *offered* since you got home. I knew you were
starting to get better. Pete said—''

''Pete? You mean Pete MacDougal? Why is he in
this conversation?''

''Nothing! No reason! None at all!''

Camille made an impatient motion. Something was
wrong with her. Every time she'd turned around for the
past four days, there was Pete, invading her thoughts,
her mind, her sleep. Naturally, she'd been denying it,
but lying to herself was getting tougher. And why
bother? When a woman was nuts, one more screw
loose hardly made any difference. ''So forget Pete. I
wasn't trying to ask you about Pete—I was only trying
to ask why you planted so much lavender. What are
you planning to do with it all.''

''Oh. Well. You know mom always grew that little
patch. The original lavender strain came from France—''

''I know Mom's history, for Pete's sake. But she
grew a few plants in a flower garden. Your stash of
lavender is about to take over the state of Vermont.''

Her sister chuckled. ''It wasn't supposed to get *that*
big. It was just...I always loved it. The scent of
lavender. The color, the texture, the look of it, everything. And right after the divorce, well, Simpson
wanted the house to live with the bimbo. And I wanted
nothing to do with him, so—''

''Vi. I know. And my offer to strangle Simpson still

stands. The point is, you wanted to start completely fresh, so you moved and came home...."

"Yeah. But when I moved here, there was really nothing specific for me to do, you know? The house was as empty as a museum, with Mom and Dad doing the retirement thing in Florida now. And for a while, the quiet was nice. I didn't have to actually find work right away, since I got a decent settlement out of the divorce, but I still had to find something to do with my time. So I just started messing with seeds and roots and strains of things."

Violet could take five hours to tell a five minute story, so Camille interrupted again. "I know. You started your Herb Haven." The store was a claustrophobic's nightmare, gobsmacked from rafters to cellar with herbs hanging upside down and herbs hanging right side up, baskets and candles and cooking herbs and medicine herbs—chokes of stuff all over the place. She didn't want to hear about it. "But you're growing acres more lavender than you could ever sell in the store, Vi."

"I guess." Violet smiled brightly. Then spooned a mound of an unidentifiable gourmet concoction on Camille's plate. "It just sort of...exploded. I started with Mom's original French lavender, mixed it with some strains Daisy sent me, then added some of my own. It was kind of like creating a kaleidoscope. A flower kaleidoscope. The strengths of one kind with the color of another with the texture of another. It was so much fun! Only I guess it's gotten a little out of hand."

"A little? Are you calling twenty acres 'a little'?"

"I never thought it would grow," Violet said defensively. "I mean, yes, I planted it. But I put it on that rocky east slope, not really thinking it had a chance of growing, but just to have something to *do* with it. I mean, that spot of land wasn't going to be used for anything because it was generally so hopeless. And the thing was, I had all these experiments in the greenhouse and they'd exploded on me. I had to have a place to put them. But I forgot...."

When her sister stopped to chew, Camille said impatiently, "You forgot what?"

"I forgot about the nature of lavender. It looks fragile and frail—but it's actually a very tough plant. In fact, it won't thrive at all if you pamper it. It has to have sun, of course, but otherwise it's happiest if you just leave it completely alone. So that dry, rocky spot actually ended up perfect for it—"

"Violet. The point is—it's everywhere."

"Oh, well. I guess. How do you like the potato salad?"

"Pardon?"

Violet motioned. "The potato salad—it's got dried lavender buds in it. I found the recipe from a really old French cookbook."

"The salad's fine." Camille's attention was diverted. "I don't want you cooking for me. Taking care of me like this." She added more clearly, "I hate it."

"I cook anyway. I like cooking. It's no trouble."

"That's not the point. The point is, I'm not your problem. I'm no one's problem." She yanked her hair back, said lowly, fiercely, "I can't work yet, Violet. I will. It's driving me crazy, living off you, not pulling my share, but—"

"Oh shut up. How many times do I have to say it? The land belongs to all of us. You know how Mom and Dad set it up. Dad's still positive that one of us will want to farm if he just waits long enough." Violet added, "And Dad's always asking how you are. If you're talking about Robert yet—"

"Don't." Camille heard the sharp slap in her tone, but couldn't help it. She wasn't talking about Robert.

"Okay, okay, take it easy." Violet fluttered to her feet, pivoted around with another dish from the counter. God knew, it was probably more fish. "You need some money?"

"No."

"Spending money. Everyone needs spending money—"

"I don't need or want anything!" She jerked to her feet at the sound of a truck engine. Someone was coming, pulling into the driveway. She all but ran to the hall for the ragged barn jacket and cap.

"Camille, come on, you don't have to run away—"

"I'm not running away. I just…" She was just having trouble breathing. Gusts of air felt trapped in her lungs, yet her heart was galloping at racetrack speeds. She didn't want to be mean to Violet. She didn't want to be mean to anyone. She just wanted to be left alone—where all that rotten moodiness wouldn't hurt anybody. Where she didn't have to work so hard to be nice, to be normal. She shoved her feet into the damp field boots and yanked at the back door—only to realize that someone was pulling the same door from the other side.

She almost barreled straight into an oak-straight, oak-hard chest. "Whoa, Cam. Easy."

Even without jerking her head up, she recognized Pete MacDougal's gentling tenor, somehow recognized the grip of his big hands steadying her shoulders.

For the briefest millisecond she just wanted to fold into his arms—big, warm, strong arms. She didn't want to fight. She just wanted to be lifted, carried, swallowed up somewhere the anger couldn't get her. But that millisecond was fleeting, of course. It was a crazy impulse, anyway.

Even a moment with Pete hit her the way it had the first time, days ago. He was a slam of strong, vital male. A reminder of what she'd lost, what she'd never have again.

She said nothing, just felt the panic squeeze tighter around her heart, and bolted past him and out the door.

He called something.

She ignored him. She ignored everything, just hurtled cross-field toward the cottage. Away from Violet. Away from Pete. Away from life.

The way she wanted it.

Three

Pete ambled out of his home office, rolling his shoulders to stretch the kinks out, and glanced at the kitchen clock. He thought it was around two. Instead, hell, it was almost three.

The boys were due home from school, and this last week in April, the kids had picked up spring fever with a vengeance. Pete knew exactly how the afternoon was going to go. The instant Sean walked in, he was going to start up with his wheedling-whine campaign to get a horse. There wasn't an animal born that boy didn't want to raise—preferably in the house. Simon was going to start in with the earsplitting music, which would get the eldest MacDougal complaining, and Ian was already having a poor-me kind of day. Laundry hadn't been done in a week, and when boys were of an age to have wet dreams, Pete had discovered that you'd best not wait too long to change the sheets and linens.

And no one had bothered with the dishes since last night, either.

The more Pete analyzed the situation, the more he realized the obvious. If he didn't run away now, the opportunity threatened to disappear. Swiftly he yanked a jacket off the hook and escaped.

Aw, man. When his lungs hauled in that first breath of fresh air, it felt like diamonds for his soul. For days it had been rainy and blustery cold, but now, finally there was some payoff. A balmy, spring breeze brushed his skin; the sun felt soft and liquid-warm. Green was bursting everywhere. Violets and trillium were coming up in the woods, daffodils budding by the fences.

He didn't realize he was hiking toward the west fence—and the border between the MacDougals and the Campbells—until he saw her. Actually, he couldn't make out exactly who was standing by that godawful lavender mess on the Campbells' east twenty acres. But someone was. A waif.

He unlatched the gate, but then just stood there. No one, but no one, had taken his heart like this in years.

Damn woman had lost so much weight that her jeans were hanging on her, the hems dragging in the dirt. She was wearing a rowdy-red shirt with a frayed neck and an old barn jacket that used to be her dad's favorite. In the sunlight, her cap of hair looked satin-black and shiny, but a shorn sheep had more style—and Pete suspected that's exactly what she'd done, taken scissors and whacked off all that gorgeous long hair after whoz-its died. Everything about her appearance told the same story. So much grief and nowhere to go with it.

Camille couldn't be his problem, he'd already told himself—several times in the past few weeks—and it was true. He had an overfilled plate now. The boys had been a nonstop handful since Debbie deserted them. Their grandfather indulged them right and left. Pete's translating work for the government had turned into a far more lucrative living than he'd ever dreamed, but come spring, he would have the land and orchards to tend on top of his real work. All in all, most days he was lucky to have a second to himself. He sure didn't need more stress.

But damn. Those eyes of hers were deep as a river.

She was looking out at those endless acres of un-tended lavender, her hands on her hips.

Pete could have sworn that he intended to turn around and skedaddle before Camille caught sight of him, but somehow he seemed to have unlatched the gate and hiked toward her instead. She startled in sur-prise when she suddenly found him standing next to her. He squinted at the fields as if they studied their respective farming problems together every day.

"Don't even start about my sister." It was the first thing she said, and in the same ornery tone she'd spo-ken to him last time.

"I thought we covered this? I always liked your whole family. Violet included. I don't think less of her because there are some raisins short in her bran. Be-cause apparently she wouldn't know a weed from a willow. Because she wouldn't recognize common sense if it bit her in the butt—"

"I've leveled guys for less, so you just quit it. There is nothing wrong with my sister."

"You don't think some of that blond hair dye seeped into her brain?"

She lifted a booted foot to kick him—then seemed to realize she'd been suckered into his teasing and stiffened up again. She took a breath, then said quietly, "Go away, Pete."

He didn't. God knew why. Maybe it was the land. Looking at all those acres of tangled, woody, gnarled growth offended the farmer in him—even if he wasn't much of a farmer anymore. "I don't know much about lavender," he admitted conversationally. "I mean, I've seen it in gardens and all, but I've no knowledge of it as a commercial crop. But a bird brain could figure out that this thicket has to be damned close to becoming completely unrecoverable—"

"It isn't your problem," Camille mentioned.

He ignored that. "The thing is, though, as bad a mess as this is…your sister started this massive planting only a few years ago. So there has to be a chance it's salvageable. Not a good chance. But at least *some* chance. The question is how and how fast. I have to believe that if you don't get control of it this spring, it'll be gone for good. Which means that about by Monday, there needs to be a crew of guys in here—"

Without turning toward him, she lifted a finger in the air. Thankfully, Pete loved a woman who could communicate without words, so he just grinned. Until he realized that she was still staring at the long stretch of wasted, woebegone fields with a determined squint in her eyes.

"Whoa. Don't even start thinking it, Cam. You can't do it. Not alone. No one could."

Finally she turned, and tipped those river-deep eyes at him. "Were you under the impression I was asking your opinion about anything?"

So sassy. So rude. So much fury.

He was tempted to kiss her. Not a little kiss, and not an old-neighbor friendly peck, either. A kiss that might shake through her anger. A kiss that might touch some of that fierce, sharp loneliness. A kiss that might make him feel better—because right now it ripped raw to watch his beautiful Camille hurting and not have the first clue how to help her.

The impulse to kiss her invaded his mind for several long seconds and stung there like a mosquito bite, itching, swelling, daring him to scratch it. Then, thank God, he came to his senses. Certainly he had his stone-headed moments—didn't everybody?—but Pete wasn't usually troubled by lunacy.

He zoned on something concrete and practical as fast as he could get the words out. "So, Cam...exactly what do you know about growing lavender?"

"Well...everyone in the family knows a little, because my mom loved it so much. She always grew enough to make sachets and soap and dried flower arrangements, that kind of thing. And Violet—she knows the recipes, all this unusual stuff about how to use lavender as a spice. And Daisy's been living in France for several years now—she knows more than both of us, because she's around Provence and the perfume industry, so she's learned how lavender's used as a perfume ingredient and all that." She added, "But what I personally know about growing lavender would fill a thimble. Assuming the thimble were extra small."

"So you know not to try and tackle all these acres by yourself." He just had to be sure she wasn't going to do anything crazy. Then he could leave. And he badly wanted to leave, before he had another damn-fool impulse to kiss her. God knew what was wrong with him. Maybe he needed an aspirin or some prune juice. For damn sure, he was going to dose himself with something when he got home—but first he needed

to be certain she wasn't determined to dive off the deep
end into a brick pool.

"Pete MacDougal. Do you really have nothing better
to do than stand around and bug me? Don't you have
a few hundred acres of apples that need pruning or
trimming or something?"

"I've got the orchards. I've also got twins—two
teenage sons—that I'm raising without their mother.
And even though everyone in White Hills think I'm a
farmer, I've been doing translating work for Langley
for a half-dozen years now, full-time. And then there's
my dad, who's been as pleasant as a porcupine ever
since my mother died." He didn't suspect she wanted
to hear any of that, but he figured he'd better give her
a frame for his life. Otherwise she had an excuse for
still treating him like a half stranger. "All of which is
to say, don't waste your breath being crabby with me.
I've got people who can out-crabby you any day of the
week, so let's get back to our conversation—"

"We're not having a conversation."

"Oh, yeah, we are. We're talking about finding a
solution for that twenty acres of lavender out there.
One possibility—and the simplest one—is a bulldozer.
I don't know if you knew Hal Wolske—"

"I'm not looking for a bulldozer. Or for help."

"Okay." He reminded himself that he came from
strong Scots stock. Which meant he had no end of patience. He might have to kick a tree, soon and hard,
but he could hold on to his patience until then or die
trying. "If you don't want to get rid of it, then you
have to find a way to make it viable. I really don't
think your sister could identify the front end of a tractor
from the back—"

"Don't you start on my sister again."

"But I do know your dad always kept two Masseys in the barn. The farmer your dad hired when he retired—Filbert Green, wasn't it?—he used to keep them well maintenanced, at least until your sis kicked him out of the job. If you want me to check them out—"

"I don't."

"Yeah, I agree, there's only so much tractors can do for you in this situation. I'm afraid what you've got is a ton of handwork. I've got a crew trimming my apples, won't be done for a couple more weeks. And they'd have to be taught what to do with the lavender. They wouldn't have a clue, but they're dependable, steady. If you want the bodies—"

"That won't be necessary, since I won't be having any strangers on the farm. I don't want your crew. Don't want anyone's crew. Don't want anyone's help or advice. Now, damn it, Pete, *stop being nice to me!*"

She whirled around to stomp off, tripped on her sagging jean hem, yanked up her trousers and *then* stomped off.

Pete didn't grin—there wasn't a damn thing funny about what shape that woman was in—but he did stand there, thoughtfully stroking his chin.

Camille had to think he was the most obnoxious jerk to ever cross her path—since she'd done everything but stand on her head to make him butt out. She didn't want help. That was obvious. She didn't want a friend. That was obvious, too.

But she'd at least roused enough to snap at him. According to her sister, that was major progress.

When a man found a wounded deer in the road, he didn't just drive by. At least a MacDougal didn't. That woman was so wounded she was over her head, sick with it, sad with it, in a rage with it. And no, she wasn't his problem, but it had been so long since a woman touched him—much less snagged a feeling from his heart—that Pete was unwilling to walk away. At least not yet.

For her sake, but just maybe, for his, too.

Camille woke up to a damp pillow, sore eyes, mental flashes in her mind of a dark alley, her screaming, Robert, the blood, the three faces of drug-crazed kids, the sick feeling of terror…

Same old same old.

She crawled out of bed and took her exasperated scowl into the bathroom. She'd just started to wash the sleep from her eyes when she suddenly heard an odd sound, coming from somewhere close to the front porch outside. A growl? Like an animal growl?

When she didn't hear it again, she assumed that she'd imagined the sound. Still, once she tugged on a sweatshirt and jeans, she glanced out the murky window in the living room—and then almost dropped the socks in her hand. As fast as she could cram on shoes, she yanked open the door.

There was a dog, tied by a rope to the maple tree. The instant it saw her, the dog sprang to its feet and lunged, starting a teeth-baring, vicious, snarling and barking routine. If it hadn't been snugly tied, Camille was pretty sure it would have been happy to tear out her throat.

Considering she was afraid of almost everything these days, she wasn't sure why the dog didn't terrify her. Possibly it was because the poor thing just looked so pitiful. It had the look of a full-blooded German shepherd—but it had obviously fallen on disastrous times. Its skinny ribs showed. Its right ear had a nip.

The eyes were rheumy, the golden-brown coat crusted with old mud.

"Take it easy, take it easy," she coaxed. But the dog showed no inclination to take it easy and snarled even harder. "Well, for Pete's sake, how did you end up here? Who tied you to my tree? What are you doing here?"

She couldn't think, the dog was barking too loudly and too fiercely. So she went back inside, shut the door, and then stared out the window. Once she was out of sight, the dog settled down. She could see a cut in its coat now, close to its right shoulder. The injury didn't appear too bad, but it was still another sign that the shepherd had been treated badly.

Unfortunately, whoever had tied it to her tree had given it enough room to run and lunge—a little—but hadn't left it food or water. How anyone had gotten close enough to bring it here to begin with, she couldn't imagine, but the mystery of the situation had to wait. She foraged in the kitchen cupboards and finally came up with a bowl. It was cracked and dusty, but it would hold water.

When she opened the door again, the shepherd leaped and lunged and did an instant replay of its snapping, snarling act. Camille hesitated, but then slowly carried the water closer. "This is ridiculous. Quit having such a cow. I'm not coming any closer than I have to—you can take that to the bank. But if you want water and food, you're going to have to shut up and relax. If you don't like me, don't worry about it. Believe me, you won't be here long."

Snarl, snarl. Growl, growl. The dog was so intent on trying to attack her that it tipped over the water bowl. Camille eased back, perplexed. What now? She couldn't free the dog—at least not without risking her life. She also couldn't leave the dog without food or water—but she couldn't seem to get water to it, and she didn't have food. Temporarily she seemed to be stymied—and confounded that this could possibly be *her* problem.

She trudged up to the main house, yanked open the back screen door and yelled for Violet. No answer. She tried upstairs, downstairs, the basement, then the front yard. No sister in any of those places, either. Finally she found Vi in the back of the second greenhouse, up to her elbows in potting soil and roots and plants. She'd look like an earth mother if it weren't for the five pounds of bangly gold bracelets and wildly tousled blond hair. The place was a jungle of earthy scents and humidity and plants that seemed to be reproducing in every direction.

"Cam!" Violet said delightedly when she spotted her. "You haven't come out here before. I never thought I'd get you to see all the stuff I've been doing in the greenhouses—"

"And I'm not here now," Camille said. "I'm here about the dog."

"What dog?"

Camille sighed. If Violet had to ask, then she obviously didn't know. "Do you have any dog food around? Or anything I could use for dog food? And do you have last night's paper?"

Asking Violet was a mistake. Once she knew the details she immediately wanted to drop everything and come help. Thankfully, a customer showed up and occupied her sister, which left Camille free to raid the farmhouse kitchen. Vi had enough cat food to feed a zoo of felines. And three days worth of newspapers, none of which listed any reference to a lost dog.

She stomped out of Violet's house, more aggravated than ever, carting a grocery bag full of dry cat food and a mixing bowl. How on earth had this come to be her problem? She couldn't care less about a dog she didn't know from stone and wasn't conceivably her responsibility.

Getting the bowl of food close to the shepherd was an uphill struggle, since it seemed to want to kill her even more than it wanted to eat. She ended up storming back up to Vi's kitchen, slamming doors around, heating up some dadblamed hamburger and driveling it into and over the cat food, then storming it back to the worthless mutt.

It quit snarling and lunging when it smelled the ground beef. The tail didn't wag, the fur didn't stop bristling, the eyes didn't look any less feral…but at least the damn dog let her push the bowl within its reach.

Then it fell on the food as if it hadn't eaten in a week, looking up and growling every few bites—but still, gulping down the chow almost without stopping to chew. By then, Camille had managed to get the heavy mixing bowl of water secured within its reach, too. God knew why she was going to so much trouble. The dog was pitiful. Too mean to love, too ugly for anyone to care, and definitely not her problem. But pitiful.

She never meant to go inside and wash windows. She hadn't done a single thing to make the cottage more livable, and still didn't plan to. But because she had to keep glancing out to check on the damned dog, the filthy windows were distracting. And once she rubbed a spot clean, the rest of the window looked disgusting. And then once one window got cleaned, the others looked beyond disgusting.

She'd used half a roll of paper towels when the dog's sudden fierce, angry barking made her jump and look out.

Pete was out there, leaning over the fence, his jeaned leg cocked forward, wearing an open-throated shirt as if it were a balmy spring day…which actually, Camille guessed it was. He was just…hanging there…looking at the dog, not appearing remotely disturbed by the canine's aggressive, noisy fury.

For just an instant, she felt the most curious fear, as if she should hide behind the door, not go out, not risk being near him again. There was an old Scottish phrase her dad sometimes used. *Ca awa.* It meant something like "proceed with caution" and that's what she thought every time she saw Pete. Something in those sexy, ever-blue eyes made her feel restless and edgy. Something in his long, lazy stride, in his tree-tall height, in those slow, teasing smiles of his made her stomach drop.

She wasn't aware of him as a man.

She couldn't be.

She certainly didn't *want* him. She didn't want anyone. She never planned to want another man as long as she lived. But damn…he did bug her.

Quickly, she shook off the ridiculous sensation. Pete MacDougal was no one she needed to feel cautious around. She knew that. He was a neighbor. He was interfering and bossy, for sure, but being afraid of him at any level was absurd. And more to the immediate point, he'd obviously noticed the dog.

So she hurled out the door lickety-split. Immediately Pete glanced up and motioned toward the shepherd.

"I see you managed to give our boy some food."

"Our boy," she repeated, abruptly realizing that Pete already knew the dog. "Peter MacDougal! You did this to me?"

"I did what?"

"You left me this dog? You tied this mean, godforsaken, dangerous dog to *my* tree? Why in God's name would you do such a thing?"

He smiled. As if she hadn't just screamed abuse on him up one side and down the other.

"His name is Darby. Used to be a show dog. Hard to believe, the way he looks now, isn't it? But he's a thoroughbred shepherd with a long, pretty lineage. The neighborhood kids used to play with him, he was that sweet and gentle...."

She crossed to the fence, her gaze sweeping the ground for a log big enough to brain him with.

"...belonged to Arthur Chapman. You remember him, don't you? Quiet guy, lived down Cooper Street and across the creek, that property on the left after the bridge. Good man. Dog lover. But then Art got Alzheimer's. Naturally, people realized he was getting strange, but you know how folks are tolerant in White Hills. So they just tried to let him be. Nobody realized that in his own house, he'd gotten mean, was beating and starving the dog. It wasn't really his fault. He wasn't in his right mind. Anyway—"

She couldn't find a log. Lots of twigs in the grass, but nothing big enough to do any damage.

"Anyway, the neighbors finally figured out that Art wasn't coping on his own. They called the cops, who called Social Services, all that. Everybody was prepared to take care of Art, but no one realized they'd find the dog in such a godawful mess.''

"You're taking this dog right back.''

"Nope, I'm not. But if you don't want him, you can call the pound.''

"I most certainly do not want him—''

"Of course, they'll put him down,'' Pete assured her genially. "They don't have the time or means to turn him around. Actually, I'm not sure anyone can. But the pound, for sure, will believe it's easier to put him to sleep. In fact, that's probably what I'd do.''

"You son of a sea dog, you take this dog back! I can't believe this! That you'd desert me. Leave me alone with this horribly vicious dog!''

"Naw. I'll give you the number for the pound, if you want them to come and kill it—''

"Quit *saying* that.''

"Quit saying what?''

"That they're going to kill the damn dog!''

"Well, Cam. That's how it is. I just thought... Darby's got one chance left. That is, if you'll give him one. He was such a great dog that I just thought, man, he has to be worth one last try.... But hell.'' Pete pushed back from the fence. "Who cares, right? I'll go home, get the phone number for the pound—''

A log was too good for him. She vaulted over the fence, determined to give him what-for. She wasn't precisely sure how to deliver that what-for, but she was madder than a bed of hornets and the "how'' didn't immediately seem that important. She hurled after him, yanked at his shirt, put a wagging finger up in his face, and the next thing she knew, she was in his arms.

It all didn't make a lick of sense. She was mad. She

knew she was mad. And whatever emotion Pete
MacDougal might have been feeling, he'd never let on
for a blink that he felt anything sexual for her.

Yet his lips came down on hers as if they had been
waiting for just that moment. His arms slid around her
waist, as if he'd known she was going to be on shaky
ground. The sun tilted in her eyes, so bright and hot
she couldn't see. She still planned to sock him. Eventually. It was just that right then...she was so stunned.

His lips were sun warmed, smooth. He dipped down
for a second kiss before she'd recovered from the first.
He was tall enough to make her feel surrounded, protected. She heard the yearning coo of a mourning dove.
Felt the damp earthy loam beneath her feet, felt the
sliver of breeze tickle the hair at her nape. She felt his
heart, beating, beating. Felt her own, clutched tighter
than a fist.

Slower than a sigh, he lifted his head. His gaze
roamed her face, his eyes dark with awareness, electric
with what they'd kindled together. She felt his fingertip
on her cheek. His voice came out rough and tender-
low.

"I knew it was in there. That soft, wonderful heart
of yours. I hate to see you hurting so bad, Cam."

He didn't lower his hand particularly fast, or turn
around and start walking away with any speed. But still
she couldn't come up with an answer before he was
already a hundred yards onto his own property. She
couldn't talk at all. She still seemed to be gulping in
air and sensation both.

There'd never been anything wrong with her IQ. She
realized perfectly well that Pete had been trying to
reach out a hand to her ever since she'd come home,
but she'd assumed it was a neighborly hand. She'd

never expected…kisses. She'd never expected to feel his heart thundering against hers, to see the stark shine of desire in his eyes, to feel his body rousing because of their closeness.

Pete wanted her.

It seemed an astounding revelation.

She stared after him, but memories of Robert suddenly pushed into her mind—her lean, elegant Robert, with his city ways and boyish grin. He'd loved the night lights. So many Friday nights they'd gone clubbing, her in her highest heels and slinkiest black dress, Robert in his city-guy clothes. Robert could dance down the house when he got in the mood; he knew his wines, knew his music, knew all the cool places to go.

Camille couldn't imagine Pete giving a damn about "a cool place" in a thousand years. He was day-and-night from Robert in every way.

Pete was lean himself, but when a man was built that tall and physical, he just wasn't…elegant. His shoulders were as broad as a trunk. His skin had an earthy tan; his hair never looked brushed. He roared when he was mad, laughed from the belly when he was happy. Nothing scared Pete. He was elemental, earthy, wild himself.

He made her think of male alpha wolves—of the kind of guy a woman was instinctively very, very careful around. Not for fear he'd hurt her, but for fear of being taken under by a force bigger than her, an emotional force, a sexual force.

Camille shivered suddenly, and then abruptly, scowled. Elemental force? Where on earth was this horse hockey coming from? The damned man had left her with a filthy, vicious dog that no one could love or want, and somehow managed to divert her attention for a couple seconds by kissing her senseless.

Well—the next time she saw him, there'd be no kisses and no nonsense either. She whirled around, only to find Killer—alias Darby—snoozing on his side in the maple's shade.

If that wasn't typical! Both males had wreaked total havoc on her day, and now one was sacked out and the other had walked away.

She was simply going to ignore them both, and that was that.

Four

When most women got kissed, Camille thought grimly, their mood perked up. At least if it had been a *good* kiss. And Pete's kiss had certainly qualified as a humdinger.

As she trudged toward the lavender fields, carrying a long-armed set of clippers, she could feel every creaky, cranky muscle in her body complaining. For three days, she'd been working nonstop in the lavender. Specifically, that was the same three days since Pete had brought her that dadblamed mangy dog and kissed her.

Working herself into a state of exhaustion hadn't made her forget Pete—but it was doing a fabulous job of completely wearing her out. It was also giving her something to do to earn her keep. The lavender appeared to be a thankless, ridiculous, hopeless job—but that just suited her mood, anyway. She wasn't looking for meaningful. She was looking for something so mind-numbing and exhausting she'd be too tired to have nightmares.

When she reached the crest of the hill, the late-afternoon sun was temporarily so blinding bright that it took several seconds before she realized she wasn't alone. There were bodies in the lavender field. Two of them. Squinting, she realized they were boys. Both were hunkered down in the first row of the overgrown lavender, working with clippers—in fact, working with far better clippers than her own.

In a single blink, she knew who they had to be. Pete's sons. They were identifiably young teenagers—at an age when boys tripped over their own feet and their arms seemed longer than their whole bodies. But she could see Pete in their height, the strong bones and ruddy skin. Both had his brown hair, too, with that hint of mahogany in the sunlight.

She clomped closer, building up a good head of steam. Obviously Pete had sent them over with the clippers. Her father would have labeled Pete a *clishmaclaver*—which was one of his Scottish terms for busybody. Doggone it, she hadn't asked for his help. And she may have turned into a rude, ornery bitch—and was proud of it!—but even a curmudgeon had to have a line. She sure as heck wasn't going to let two young boys kill themselves working in those hopelessly overgrown twenty acres.

"Boys! Hey!" She yelled, the instant she was within hearing distance. It wouldn't take her two seconds to send them both packing; she was sure of it.

They both immediately jerked upright. "Hey, Ms. Campbell!" Damn, but they were startlingly alike. Except one had a cowlick—the same one who pushed a step forward, with an agonizing-red blooming on his cheeks as if he normally died from having to speak to strangers. "Hi, Ms. Campbell, I saw the dog in your yard."

She still intended to throw them both off the property, but obviously that comment forced her to recognize a greater priority—their safety. "Good grief—you guys didn't try to go close to Killer, did you?"

"No," the shy one spoke up again. "I meant—I saw what you did with the snow fence. Making a yard for him and all. That was cool. Giving him a way to get some exercise so he didn't always have to be tied up."

Camille perched a fist on her hip. She didn't need praise from some baby-aged kid for hauling five tons of snow fence, all to create a stupid yard for a mangy, worthless, violently aggressive mutt who hated her and everyone else. She needed someone to give her a whack upside the head for being so crazy. But before she could correct the boy's misconception of her, his brother pushed ahead of him. This one was just as good-looking and gawky, but he didn't have a cowlick—and no shy blush on his cheeks. "We shoulda said who we were. I'm Simon. That's Sean. Sean's the one who found Darby. Dad says he's always finding trouble."

"Am not."

"Are, too." Simon poked him, then kept talking as if the two of them regularly conducted conversations while socking each other. "See, we heard about Mr. Chapman being taken to a rest home. But it's like nobody remembered that he had a dog, until Sean did. Mr. Gaff let us in the house. Sean found Darby in the back room, locked in, all dirty, no food, no water. He'd turned wild like. In fact, I thought he was gonna kill

Sean. Not that that wouldn't be a good riddance and all—"

Sean slugged him. Simon slugged back. Camille rubbed two fingers on her temples, wondering when and how she was going to throw them off the property, when so far she couldn't even get a word in.

And Simon kept right on talking, even as he was being slugged. "Anyway, the pound loaned us this leash they use on wild or sick animals. It's like any other leash, except that it has this stick thing attached so the dog can lunge, but not so close he can bite you. Anyway, then Sean brought it home—"

Sean finally ventured another comment. "—And Simon's gonna tell you that Dad was mad at me. Which he was. But it's like no biggie. Dad always has a cow when I bring home another animal. The point is that Dad figured out right away that you'd be the perfect person to adopt Darby."

Camille's jaw dropped. "Your dad said what?"

"He said you'd be the one person who could save Darby. I mean, I could save him, too. But we've already got dogs and cats and raccoons and homing pigeons and all, and like, obviously, Darby is too ornery right now to be around other animals. So we couldn't take him. There was just no way. And that's when Dad said you were the perfect one. Because you were the only one in White Hills who was even meaner than Darby."

Again her jaw dropped. "He said *what?*"

"Yeah, cool, huh? I wasn't convinced, because you're a woman and all. But then Dad explained that you're not really like a woman."

This time her voice seemed to raise a complete octave. *"He said what?"*

The brothers exchanged glances, as if suddenly aware she didn't sound thrilled with the conversation. The one without the cowlick—Simon—seemed to be inherently elected to handle difficult verbal situations with adults. "Dad said you're okay. Like, look at you. You dress like a guy. You've got dirty boots. Your hair's all messed up. You're ornery. I mean, you're practically like us."

Sean nodded, as if anxious to clear up this problem of potentially offending her. "See, once Mom took off, we all just said screw it. We don't need or want women in our lives, you know? Because Dad was, like, way depressed. And now he's fine. The whole trick was getting rid of women."

Simon finished up the explanation. "Now do you get us? If you were like a woman, we'd never have trusted you to take Darby."

"I see." Actually, what Camille saw was that a chill wind was scooching over the hill; it was nearing the dinner hour; she hadn't gotten a lick of work done; and now she had to translate fourteen-year-old-teenage-boy lingo into something an adult might understand. That godforsaken dog was clearly a prize. To them. And that she was apparently too unkempt and ornery to be "like a woman" was a giant compliment. To them.

"Okay. Anyways…" Both boys suddenly turned around and picked up their clippers again.

"Whoa. Wait a minute there—"

"It's okay, Ms. Campbell. We know what to do. Dad called the county extension office, and this guy talked to all of us about lavender, how it's grown, what to do and everything."

"We know it's a flower. Neither of us wanted to

work around anything sissy like flowers, but it's not your fault, after all, that your sister's so bonkers—''

"Simon, shut up. You're insulting her family, you nimwit."

"Oh." Simon glanced back, stricken. "Hey, I didn't mean anything. I meant to say how sorry I was for you. Your sister scares all of us, and you have to deal with her all the time. It can't be easy."

"Anyways…" Sean started *clip, clip, clipping* as he talked. "We learned a bunch of junk. It was pretty interesting, about how there's English lavender and French lavender and Spanish lavender. What you got here is apparently all kinds of crossbreeds."

"And what we have to do is lop off about a third from the top and sides." Simon glanced at her clippers, shook his head. "Yours aren't sharp enough. They have to be good ones. But back to the job. We have to cut the stems back to a few inches from where the woody part starts. See?"

He motioned, and stayed hunkered down like that until she came over, scowling, and bent down to have a look. Then he went on. "This is like a big mess. It'll take three years to get it back, the county guy said, but you can do it if it's worked right. Lop the sides and top. Then the stems back. Then next year, you do another third. Then by the third year, it'll be vible again."

"Vible?"

"Vi-*a*-ble," Sean said disgustedly. "He gets Cs in English. He's so stupid."

"Am not."

"Are, too. Anyways, Ms. Campbell, you really got a lot of this lavender."

She tried wildly waving a hand to get a turn in. "I know I do, but I don't need you boys!"

They stopped working abruptly, but both of them looked crushed. "Dad's paying us, Ms. Campbell, so you don't have to. And it's either this or we have to clean the bathrooms and do the wash. I mean, come on. We really work good. I promise. And we can get here most afternoons by like three-fifteen or so. You wouldn't fire us before you even gave us a chance, would you?"

For Pete's sake. She'd like to throw up on the whole damn world, but how was she supposed to be mean to two motherless brats? "You two can't possibly do this whole twenty acres and that's that. You can work for an hour in the afternoon sometimes. IF you want to. *When* you want to. And only if it doesn't interfere with your damned schoolwork, you hear me?"

Yup, they both heard her. They were both nodding like bobbing corks.

"And I never said 'damned' either!"

More exuberant nodding. Hell. It was all she could do not to slick down Sean's cowlick and jog up to the house to bring cookies to the brats.

She stormed back to the cottage, thinking that this just wasn't going to work. She knew it. But this was Pete's doing, so the only way she could stop it was to go directly to Pete.

And that meant risking being near him—not that he'd want to kiss her again. Considering that he apparently thought of her as an unkempt, ugly, genderless nonwoman, it was astounding that he'd wanted to kiss her the first time. Nevertheless, once you'd been stung by a mosquito, you knew what the itch was like and obviously avoided it a second time if you could.

She could put up with the boys. For a while. Anything was better than risking getting too close to Pete again—at least until she figured out what the Sam Hill that kiss had been about.

Camille waited the dog out for three more days, but by Saturday afternoon, she'd had it. When the temperature climbed to a reasonably warm seventy-six degrees, she pulled on ragged shorts and a black tee, then carted outside a bucket, flea shampoo, rags and a hose.

Killer—alias Darby—had been allowing her to bring food and water, particularly if the food included ground round, and he'd quit snarling in her presence. But coming close enough to touch him was a different proposition. He bared his teeth when she stepped off the cottage porch, and bristled into a hair-ruffed growl when she got within five feet.

She stopped there. Temporarily. "Look," she said irritably. "You stink. You stink so bad I can smell it through the windows. I've had it with this whole attitude thing. If you think you can out-mean me, buster, you've got another think coming. Now you're getting a bath today, and I mean to tell you, that's that."

Growl, snap, snarl. Growl, snap, snarl.

Camille pushed back her hair, put her hands on her hips, and growled right back. Her voice was deceptively as soothing as a whisper. "You want to tear me apart?" she demanded. "Well, where you're making a mistake, Killer, is thinking that I care. If you were a person, my dad would be calling you a *sumph*. You know what that is? In Scottish, it's the word for a half-wit. Because that's how you're behaving. Half-witted."

She'd been talking to him for days, knowing he was completely ignoring her, but she didn't turn her back on the dog. She wasn't that stupid. Quietly she bent down, added the flea shampoo to the warmish water in the bucket, and dunked in the rag. Killer stopped snarling—until she took another step closer—and then he resumed the fierce warning growls.

"I am *so* sick of this. You snap at me, I'll snap right back, you no-count worthless mutt. You think life's treated you so terribly? Well, big frigging deal. I lost everything...." When he stopped growling, she took a quiet step toward him.

"So the owner you loved turned mean and now you don't trust anyone. That's tough. Real tough." She took another step. Then another. "But the guy I loved was killed by strangers. The court system barely slapped their hands. I'll never feel safe again as long as I live. I literally lost everything—my job, my husband, my life. Myself." Calmly, slowly, she sponged the soapy water on his neck and back. The dog went still, rigid as stone, eyes tracking her with the fierceness and anger of a predator. "So don't waste that stupid attitude on me. I'm tired of it. You think life's unfair? I agree. You think life's not worth living? I agree. You just want to be left alone to be miserable—man, I agree with that, too. And I'll leave you completely alone. But you have to have a bath first, because I'm the one trying to sleep under that window there. I've been living with that smell ever since you got here. I've had enough..."

It wasn't as if she were sweet-talking the darn dog. She was being plenty mean and tough. She just happened to be using a crooning tone of voice, because as long as she kept talking, he stopped growling and was letting her wash him. Maybe he was just sick of being filthy, who knew? But her heart was beating hard enough to implode—it wasn't easy getting this close to the dog, when she had every reason to fear it might attack her. Still. She had to try something. The wild, despairing rage in its eyes—she couldn't stand it anymore. She understood it. All too well.

"I'm not going near your face or eyes, so don't get your liver in an uproar. Just a little more now. Then I'll rinse you off and leave you alone. I'll be darned, I thought you were almost all brown. But you're more than half blond, aren't you, you low-down, ornery—"

From behind her, she heard the sound of a gate unlatching.

"…boneheaded, pea-brained, worthless…"

And then she heard the quiet clomp of a boot on her porch.

"…lazy, stubborn…. DAMN IT, KILLER!" She had a pretty good grip on the dog, but her hands and the dog's coat were both slippery, and suddenly Killer bolted, knocking over the bucket of soapy water. On her. Followed by his shaking all over. On her. And then the dog just stood there, staring at her, sopping wet with his tongue hanging out. As if they were friends. As if he'd forgotten all about wanting to rip her throat out and how much he hated her and all humans and everything else.

And then she heard another sound coming from behind her…the rumble of a man's throaty, wicked, *evil* laughter.

Whew. Pete tried to choke back the laugh, because she turned on him faster than a man could spit.

"What's so funny, Pete MacDougal?"

He cocked a foot forward. "You. Saw a cat fall in a well once. It didn't look half as drowned as you do." Well, that was a complete lie. She was wet, yes, but she looked damned adorable, with her spiky hair and the animation and color in her cheeks. More to the point, she'd broken his heart with how much she'd revealed about herself when she was talking to the dog. And broke his heart more, seeing her still trying, so hard, to be tough, to not feel or care, when it was as obvious as sunshine she cared so much she was crying from the weight of it.

"Dadblamit, MacDougal! I'm not going to take any more insults from you!"

He blinked. "Actually, I just got here, so really, I've only had a chance to insult you once. And then, what can I say? You *are* wetter than the dog. Got more suds and mud on you than the dog twice over. But I don't recall say anything else—"

"Well, you didn't. Today. But you sure filled your boys' ears last week!"

She shot past him so fast he didn't have a chance to register more than a "Huh?" More interesting, since she'd neglected to forbid him inside the door, he trailed in after her.

Years ago, he'd seen the inside of the cottage. A great-grandmother had lived there for years, had still been around to hand out cookies and candy at Halloween when he'd been a kid. He remembered the place as being small, but full of color and light.

Now the whole fireplace wall was stacked to the ceiling with moving boxes—Pete assumed that Camille still hadn't unpacked from Boston. The windows looked washed, but otherwise the level of dust rivaled his sons' housekeeping. He saw boxes for fancy kitchen equipment, like the latest in coffeemakers and pasta makers and toast makers and all those other "makers"—yet none of that was unpacked. In fact, through the doorway of the old-fashioned kitchen, he could see a battered stainless coffeepot on the old stove that was too pitiful to be called an antique.

So she was still camping out. Still not actually living anywhere. At least emotionally.

Pete pushed a hand through his hair, waiting. Camille had disappeared into the bedroom—he could hear her muttering through the half-closed door. Eventually he saw a soggy lump of cloth hurled on the floor, followed by another.

When Cam finally reemerged, she was barefoot but at least dry, wearing worn jeans and a dry shirt. It was another one of those shirts that must have been her dad's, because the old blue chambray looked soft as a baby's butt, frayed and shapeless.

He hadn't figured out yet whether she was trying to be as ugly as possible, or if she was unconsciously trying to cover herself with comforting things—like the clothes that had belonged to her father.

Pete could have told her that the ugly goal was completely unattainable and doomed to failure. Those dark eyes and pale skin and that soft, vulnerable mouth took his breath every time he saw her. But that she might be trying to cover herself with comforting things made him think about her father. Colin Campbell was a good guy. Pete had always thought of him as an honorary uncle, although he hadn't seen him since the Campbells retired and moved south. Colin, though, had always been a strong, protective father with his daughters—so much so that Pete wondered if her dad even realized how much pain his baby daughter was in.

Of course, try to be nice to her and you could get your head bitten off. He knew better than that—so when she showed back up in the doorway, he said immediately, ''What were you talking about, implying that I'd filled my boys' ears about you? What did they tell you? That I'd put you down in some way?''

"Not exactly. Just forget it." She didn't flip him a finger, which Pete thought was progress. And she was carrying a brush, which also seemed to be progress, a sign that she cared what her wild thatch of thick, short hair looked like—except that she shook the brush at him en route to her kitchen. "I don't want your sons helping me with the lavender."

"You don't like my boys?" Immediately he stiffened.

"I don't like anyone, so don't take it personally. Your boys are terrific. Although if I were you, I'd get the damn horse for Sean before he nags you into an early grave. And don't be telling Simon any secrets, because he'll tell anyone anything—"

"Yeah, in fact, I already heard from Simon that you've been feeding them delicacies they never get at home."

"That's a complete lie. I only brought them some sandwiches and stuff because they were working so hard," she said defensively. "And because they're boys. And being boys, they seem to be hungry all the time."

Obviously she thought he'd accused her of being kind, because the teakettle got slammed in the sink. And once the kettle was filled, it got slammed on the stove. And then a mug got slammed on the counter. One mug. He couldn't help but notice that she didn't offer him any.

"I haven't starved either kid. I swear. No matter what they told you," he said deadpan.

She rolled her eyes. "The point is, that I don't want them working on the farm. I mean it, Pete. It's not right, unless I could pay them. And I positively can't afford to pay them.''

"I've been paying them—"

"I know that. And it's even more wrong. I don't want your charity, and the whole lavender thing isn't your problem.''

"Okay, I know how to settle this," Pete said peaceably. "I'll go ask your sister—"

As expected, she promptly paled in horror, and dropped a spoon. "Come on. Don't sic Violet on me. That's not fair.''

He scratched his chin. "Well, see, there we have a problem. Because I either have to talk to your sister or to you. There are some decisions that have to be made on all that lavender. I have to ask one of you before going ahead—"

"What in God's name are you trying to interfere with now?'' she asked, obviously exasperated. In fact, so exasperated that she seemed to blindly set down a second mug in front of him. And once the hot water bubbled, she even stirred in some instant coffee for him.

He took a sip of the sludge. Her coffee was almost—almost—as bad as his. "Well, there are three things we have to decide. The first is, your sis is going to have to invest in mulch, because you've got good drainage there, but not good enough for lavender. Then, assuming you actually want to make something of that mess, you need soil with a pH around six point five, which I haven't tested for. But I suspect—knowing the nature of my land next to that acreage—that you're going to need to side dress the plants with some lime.''

He watched her sink into the scarred chair across the table. Violet's eyes would have crossed at the first mention of soil pH and lime. Not Camille's. She not only knew land; she had a sense for it that neither of her sisters had. It was pretty obvious, though, that she hadn't thought through the long-term dimensions of the lavender problem. Still, she responded swiftly. "I can do all that without help."

"Yeah?" He figured she had the strength to mulch twenty acres like a cow could fly.

"I can, Pete."

"Uh-huh." At one time, the little kitchen had been a cheerful oasis. Now, the sink had rust stains; the paint was peeling and the floor needed to be redone.

"You think my dad raised a couch potato? Maybe it's been a few years, but I know how to fertilize and mulch and all. I just didn't…"

"You didn't know the lavender was going to need it. And neither, apparently, did your sister. She's not a couch potato either, but as far as I know she never steps into a field if she can help it. Which brings us to our main problem—"

"There is no *our*, MacDougal." When he sipped his coffee and said nothing, she prodded him, "So? So? What is this big problem supposed to be?"

Pete raised a hand. This was a serious question, no teasing. "I have to know what she's trying to do. Your sister. I mean, I read up on lavender, so I'd get an idea why anyone'd grow the darn stuff. But it's not as if Violet planted a little flower garden here. Apparently she bred and crossbred all kinds of varieties. In France, now, lavender's a major crop in the perfume industry— but it's about the oil, not about the flower. Unless your sister planned to grow enough flowers for all the florists in the entire northern hemisphere, I have to assume she was hoping to harvest the oil. Only I don't see any harvesting equipment to extract the oil. I don't even know if she's looked into potential markets. There's only so much money you can pour into this if—"

"I hear you. I'll sit on my sister and find this stuff out." Camille had seemed to be listening, but suddenly she blurted out, "When'd she leave you, Pete?"

"Huh?"

"Your ex-wife. When did she leave you and the boys? I figured it couldn't have been long ago, because the hurt seems pretty fresh. The boys really talk up how much they don't miss her. How much they don't love her. How much they don't care."

Pete chugged down the coffee, but only so he could set the mug down. He hadn't come here to talk about this. "Yeah, well, it's been a couple years. Almost three. It's my dad who feeds them that kind of anti-women talk, making out like it's fun to live like bachelors, not need women, all that. You know my dad."

"I used to."

"So you know he adored my mom. Nothing anti-women about him. I don't understand why he keeps pushing the attitude on the boys. It seems as if he thinks we'll all be hurt less if we just pretend we don't need women in our lives."

"They really do seem like good kids, Pete."

"They are. But it's always there, you know? Hiding in the closet. That their mom left them. That she loved them so little that she could just take off and not look back. Reality is, she took off on *me*, not them. But that's not how kids see it." Pete frowned. He wasn't sure why he was spilling all this stuff. He couldn't remember talking this much about Debbie or the divorce. To anyone.

And Camille was suddenly frowning right back at him. "It's none of my business."

"Actually—it isn't."

She was on her feet faster than a flash. "It's not as if I care. I only started this whole conversation to tell you that I didn't want your help, or your boys' help, or anyone else's help."

He stood up, too, thinking the damn woman was more mercurial than a summer wind. For a minute there, she'd not only listened about the scope of the lavender problems—which she sure as hell had no way to know about, coming in cold to the farm after all this time. But she'd also asked about his sons and the divorce situation as if she actually cared. Without thinking, he murmured, "I keep getting glimpses of the Camille I remembered. The Camille you used to be."

Wrong thing to say. Scarlet streaked her cheeks faster than fire. "Well, I'm not that person. That girl's gone forever and never coming back, so if you were thinking—"

"I wasn't thinking anything, so don't be tearing any more bloody strips off me." His voice dropped low. Lower than a bass tenor and quieter than midnight. "Cam, I understand anger. If I'd been through what you have, I'd be tearing the bark off trees. I'm sorry you've been through such hell. But I'm not part of anything that hurt you. I'm just an old friend who happens to have the means and time to help you with the lavender. And I've got two sons who are teenagers, which means they're selfish as hell, and that means it'll do *them* good—for *their* sakes—to put in some hours doing something for someone besides themselves. Now, that's all that's going out there, so quit giving me a *murdle-grups*."

Her father used to use that Scottish term—*murdle-grups*. It meant bellyache. And Pete thought using it might make her smile. But apparently she'd scared herself, having a conversation with him as if she cared. She didn't want to care. Not about him. Which she seemed obligated to make crystal clear.

Her chin went up a notch. "I'm not keeping the dog."

"No?"

Her chin shot up another defiant inch. "I've been tending him. I admit that. But I've only been taking care of him because I didn't want him put away. The very instant he's better, I'm finding him a home and getting rid of him."

"You do that. That'll show me how mean you are," he goaded her.

"I *am* mean."

Aw, hell. It was such a stupid conversation that he couldn't think of a single reason to continue it. So he grabbed her and kissed her instead.

What else could he possibly have done? She was just standing there, fists on her hips, looking like a waif against Goliath. She wasn't going to quit challenging him unless he did something.

This time, though, she knew his kiss.

She knew the taste of him.

She knew the risk of him.

And for damn sure, Pete knew how much trouble she was. Or he thought he did.

Before he'd severed the first kiss, he was already coming back for another, his fingers disappearing into her thick, damp hair, his body picking up her body heat—even through the huge shirt she was wearing. Her impossibly soft skin was another aphrodisiac pull—and he didn't need any more pulls. She was already yanking every emotional chain he had.

He'd managed without since Deb left. No question that he was more primed than a lit stick of dynamite, but in all this time, it was easier doing without than volunteering for any more wear-and-tear on his heart.

He knew, instinctively, that Camille would risk more wear-and-tear than maybe his heart could handle.

But she kissed like the loneliest soul he knew. She kissed as if he were her first. As if she was shaky-scared and still couldn't turn away. As if she was starved to touch and be touched, to hold and be held. As if she'd die if he let her go.

One kiss seeped into another, whispered into another, danced into another. A counter jammed into his back as he pulled her closer in, dipping down for another slower, deeper kiss. His fingers trailed down, kneading her shoulders, then molding down her back. Her breasts tightened, snugged against him so he could feel her bare nipples, smell the perfume of her skin, feel the frantic beat of her heart.

He found her soft, silken lips again. Heard the murmur of a groan deep inside her throat when he took her tongue. Her responsiveness caused his pulse to jackhammer. He lifted her tighter, higher, closer to him, nestling her between his thighs.

She kissed back like a summer storm, all heat and lightning and surprise. Hell. How could such a small package have been hiding so much explosive passion?

He thought: it wasn't that she wanted him. It was that she'd been alone so long. He thought: it couldn't be that he mattered to her, because half the time she was furious with him. In his head he understood—really understood—that this wasn't likely about him.

She'd just been so lost since her husband died that being kissed and desired opened a door that had been rusted shut with grief and pain.

But just then, just for that minute, he sucked in those hot, wet kisses of hers. Inhaled the lush feeling her busy hands invoked. Smelled her skin, inhaled the earthy sweet sounds of longing she made. At least until she nipped his neck.

And then his eyes bolted open and he lifted his head with a little shock—and humor. "You bit me," he murmured.

"What can I say? I missed lunch."

"But you. *You*. Actually bit me."

"You're telling me a woman's never taken a nip of you before, MacDougal? What, have you been with all sissies?"

"Campbell, are you flirting with me? From the minute you came home, you've given me grief nonstop."

"It wasn't personal. I've given everyone grief. Temporarily, though, all I can think about is having you for lunch."

Nobody have given him a sudden ticket to Never Never Land. Reality was all around him. The silky sunlight. The dust. The sound of birdsong. The smells of bad coffee and verdant earth and flowering almond outside the window screen. Yet all he could see was her wildly tumbled hair, the ache in her eyes, her mouth swollen from his kisses. Her face was still, her gaze searching his just as urgently as his searched hers.

"What's going on here?" he asked gently.

"Maybe I'm trying to scare you away."

"And you think I'll scare?"

Silence. Then she touched his cheek with her fingertip. "Yeah, I do, Pete. I don't know why you keep kissing me. I don't know why you keep trying to help me. But you have to know that I'm a walking catastrophe. I can't fit in your life, in your sons' life. I'm not ready for any kind of relationship. I'm not ready for much of anything.''

''Yeah. So?''

A whisper of a grin, the first natural one he'd seen on her lips. ''Don't get sassy with me, you dolt. I'm serious. If you come on to me, you could get what you're asking for. Trouble. So you think it through real good before you kiss me again, you hear?''

Slowly, she pulled completely free from his arms, then turned around and simply walked out. The screen door clapped behind her.

The damn woman had left him in her kitchen. And he stood there for a good five minutes, feeling as dazed as if someone had smacked him upside the head—or upside the heart. God knew what he was going to do about her. Right then, for sure, he didn't have a clue.

Five

Nothing had gone well for the entire week, and as far as Camille was concerned, it was all Pete's fault. He'd rattled her. It was one thing for her high school crush—the heroic icon of her whole darn childhood—to turn into a living, breathing man who seemed to be attracted to her. But entirely another thing for her to respond to him.

Obviously there was nothing serious between them—and couldn't be. It was just a matter of shaking off this constant rattled feeling. So she'd withdrawn. Specifically, she tried holing up in the cottage the way she had those first weeks, but that no longer seemed to work. The darn dog took all kinds of time and care. And the lavender simply had to be tended. And then, Pete's boys kept showing up to help her.

Camille was all for denial and cowardice and hiding

out, but dagnabbit, a woman couldn't even be a neurotic hermit in peace around here.

She hiked the driveway between the main house and her sister's Herb Haven business. Clouds had started building before noon, and now they were chasing across the sky, tumbling over each other, bringing a storm in their shadows. Since she'd been chased out of the lavender field because of the inclement weather, she figured she might as well use the time to suck it up and seek out her sister.

She hoped to find Violet alone, but when she poked her head in the Herb Haven, she spotted at least three bodies wandering around—that is, three human bodies, not counting the half-dozen cats.

She shied from the sound of strangers' voices. She'd have shied from the cats, too, except that two of the long-haired Persians tangled around her legs before she could escape back outside. Trying to walk to the greenhouses was an exercise in getting tripped and sabotaged. Finally, she hunched down to pet them, snarling behind her, "Dammit, Killer. You're a dog. Isn't it a mandate that you're supposed to chase cats? What good are you?"

She didn't have to look back to know the shepherd was as close behind her as bad breath. Killer was still snarling at every opportunity—including at her—but this last week, he'd taken up following her everywhere. She couldn't go to the bathroom, couldn't go to dinner, couldn't close the door on her bedroom without him. Just like now, he sat patiently, tongue lolling, less than two feet away from the disgusting sight of her petting the two long-haired nuisance cats.

The damn dog was just like having a second conscience. Couldn't escape him for love or money.

Finally the cats seemed sated. She stood up, slugged her hands in her jeans pockets, and wandered around the first greenhouse. Her parents had built this one. It wasn't as high-tech as Vi's new greenhouse, but it still had touches of their mother in here—Margaux's sacred pruning shears, her tidy potting sink and counter, the old French apron she used to wear.

Camille swallowed hard. Margaux was a wildly flamboyant flower lover, like Violet. And like Daisy. Cam was the only misfit of the daughters, the only one who'd wanted a high-stress city job, the one who'd never loved romantic lace and doodads. But when she was in here, sometimes she imagined the faint hint of her mother's perfume, lavender and jasmine, the warm scents hiding in all the musky, humid greenery.

Of course, that was foolishness. The greenhouse smelled like dirt and fertilizer, nothing more fanciful than that. She didn't miss her mother. She was long a grown woman, for God's sake. She was just...ticked off. Because she'd postponed talking to Violet as long as she possibly could—not because she cared about what her sister was going to do with the lavender, but because she'd promised Pete.

And darn it, she definitely didn't want to think about Pete.

So she poked and prodded, sniffed flowers, tested soil, read labels, snooped. By the time she heard Violet's exuberant, "Hey, you!" she'd explored one greenhouse stem to stern and was halfway through the new one.

"Cam! You're out and about. Still with the mutt, I see." Violet sidestepped Killer, who growled and snarled for a second, but Vi had stopped being impressed by the dog's shenanigans. She barely spared him a patient look before surging forward. Today she was wearing one of her floppy straw hats, a peasant blouse and a gypsy skirt printed with every color and some that probably didn't exist. "You could have found me in the store if you needed me."

"You had customers. And I wasn't in any hurry."

"You mean, you're still avoiding talking to anyone. Have you been to town yet? Even once?" Vi glanced at her face and said hastily, "Never mind, never mind. I'm so glad you're here. Did you see my peonies? My St. John's Wort? How about this one? You know what this is?"

She pointed to a silver-leaved plant, flowering now with deep, deep blue petals and bright yellow stamens. Camille figured she'd better cater to her. "No, what is it?"

"Nightshade. There are different kinds of wild nightshade. This silver-leafed one is poisonous, but it's also a wonderful, healing herb. People shouldn't be afraid of it. I mean potatoes and tomatoes are cousins of nightshade, and we all love those. And over here, Cam. Do you know what this one is?"

Camille had barely settled down to study the night-shade before Vi was dancing off, all excited now, fluttering from plant to plant like a butterfly. "Are you looking?" Violet demanded.

"Yes. Sheesh." Truth to tell, most things in the greenhouses were gorgeous, but the plant Violet motioned to now was uglier than a weed. The leaves were coarse and stiff and fuzzy.

"It's called a button bush. Reminds me of lavender."

"Are you kidding? Lavender's beautiful. This looks something you'd spray to kill."

"Well, I know it's not much to look at. But you can't pamper lavender and you can't pamper this either. Lavender's going to grow where it's going to grow. It's like a Scot. You can't tell it anything. This button bush'll grow, but only if you create kind of the same marshy, hostile environment where it grows naturally."

"And you'd do that why?" Camille asked wryly.

"Because it's so pretty in dried bouquets. And that's a lot of why people want herbs. Some for medicine or healing. Some like flowers. Some want them for spices. But some just like to dry them, and these buttons really add something cute in a bouquet."

"Okay." Camille interrupted before her sis could go on another endless tangent. "I looked around. Everything you're doing is cool, Vi. It's interesting. But you actually think there's a chance of selling all this stuff? The greenhouses are jammed full."

"Yeah, they are, aren't they…" Vi connected nozzles. Started sprays. Pinched a brown leaf here and there. Kept on the move. "I don't know. I mean, I haven't really added up stuff in the ledgers for a while. There hasn't been time. But I had money from the divorce."

"I knew the creep gave you a decent settlement, but I guess I thought you'd want to sock it away, for savings. Security."

"Maybe I should have saved some. But after the divorce, I just needed to make something instead of destroy something, you know? Build something instead of splitting it apart. And when I got into breeding these plants, learning how to propagate them, watching all the new babies emerge like a surprise…it was so *wonderful*."

"It is wonderful, Vi." Camille hadn't had to be tactful—or tried to be tactful—in months now. If she could have ripped any hint of softness from her character, she would have. But somehow she sensed there was something going on with her sister that she didn't understand, so she tried to tread more carefully. "But, all the new breeds of lavender you started out there…did you realize how much you were planting?"

"Well. Sort of."

"Vi, you're going to have enough lavender to stock the East Coast. You can't possibly sell even a portion of it just in your Herb Haven. You must have researched other markets? For the oil? And florists? And—?"

"I will, I will, Cam." Her sister rushed closer to snuggle her in a fast, warm hug, then drew back with a beaming smile. "Don't worry about the silly old lavender. Who cares? I'll figure out all that marketing stuff. I just want you to get rested and get well. And you are feeling better, aren't you?"

"I'm fine. I was always fine," Camille said impatiently.

Violet, when you never expected it, could suddenly turn heartless. "So, since you're so fine, that's that. We're going out to dinner tonight. In White Hills."

Panic slicked up Camille's pulse, slippery as a snake and twice as icky. "No, I—"

"Come on, Cam. We'll have a girls' night out. Don't you remember how many times you and me and Daisy would do that, go into town, shop or have dinner on any excuse—and how much fun we always had? Come on! We can go pig out on something decadent. Eat chocolate. Drink wine. And how about a movie?"

"NO. I mean it! No!" She spun around and hustled for the greenhouse door, Killer hurtling right after her.

Violet sighed. "Cam. I love you, sis. But you either do this with me, or I'm going to have to get tough."

"Don't you call mother!"

"Hey. I'm not that low. But I am warning you—"

Camille kept on going. Vi had threatened to tell on her before, but she hadn't. Violet wouldn't easily worry Mom or Dad any more than she would. Both of them would tattletale a problem with Daisy, but with Daisy still living in France for now, Camille felt safe from her interference, too. Besides, she'd get off the farm. When she got around to it. Some time. Eventually.

A blustery storm came and went, making Cam pace like a caged mouse. The instant the rain stopped, she took off with clippers for the lavender field, with Killer hugging her shadow.

Determinedly, she began pruning and clipping, pruning and clipping. The sky occasionally dripped, and the gloomy light seemed infused with a gray-damp chill. But, it was easier to work in cool than heat, even though some of the injuries from the attack came back to haunt her. Her ribs ached sharply if she clipped too fast; her ankle tried to give out if she pushed too hard— and God knows, she'd been pushing herself to the point of blisters.

Still, especially this afternoon, the work was exactly what she needed. Each lavender bush needed to be framed into a ball shape, but every single cut affected every single other cut. The work took just enough concentration that she didn't have spare time to think or brood.

When she suddenly heard the sound of a truck engine charging down the farm road behind her, she immediately stood up. It was a white pickup, the newer kind of truck style with a back seat and back doors, and yes, of course she recognized it. But where she'd become used to seeing the two younger MacDougals, her heartbeat thumped like a fretful puppy's tail at the sight of Pete.

Although he pulled up and braked, he took his time before climbing out. For a moment he just sat there, his arm resting in the open window, looking terrific in an open-throated shirt, his face freshly shaved, his hair brushed. Something in his eyes made her think of un-banked fires and unfinished kisses, and worried her heartbeat all over again.

Still, it was his boys who exploded out of the truck. Par for the course, they looked like refugees from a rascal camp, hair all over the place, tripping as they galloped toward her in pants that sagged below their shoes.

They both yelled, "Hey, Camille!" as if they were delighted to see her, when the damn boys knew perfectly well she'd been churlish and rude to both of them. She frowned as they sprinted toward her, noting that Killer opened his eyes but didn't waste any energy barking or snarling for either of them.

"You gotta come with us!" Sean reached her first, panting since he'd run the lavender rows at a breakneck pace.

"Yeah, we're going to dinner and a movie. But we only get to go if you come."

"Whoa," Camille said firmly, thinking that she was going to strangle her sister and not look back. She'd *trusted* Vi. Sure, sisters threatened each other—that's what sisters did—but damnation, she'd never thought Violet would sink so low as to sic an outsider on her.

Telling Daisy or mom on her would have been loathsome. But sheesh. Tattletaling to Pete was low-down mean.

"It's a school night," Simon explained. "Which means that we usually never get to do anything. Much less go to a movie. Much less go out to dinner and not have to do dishes. And Gramps is going to play euchre with his friends, so he doesn't need us at home."

"Well, that's nice. But you don't need me to come with you."

"Dad says we do. Dad says, if we can get you to go, then fine. Otherwise we have to go back home and do dishes and homework. Come *on*, Camille."

"Yeah, come on. The future of our world rests with you. You want us to have to go home and wash *dishes?* I mean, is that fair?"

She wasn't just going to kill her sister. She was going to feed her sister to red ants. On a hot day. After Violet had been slathered with honey.

Camille pushed at her hair. "Look, guys. I feel your pain. I think dishes are a fate worse than death, too. But I'm not going anywhere. You don't need me. I've been working outside. My hands are dirty. I've been in these jeans all day. I—"

"Like, so?" Sean said in confusion.

To a woman she wouldn't have to explain. "So I can't go out in public like this."

"That's dumb," Simon informed her. "We like how you look. You look like one of us.

She wanted to pinch the bridge of her nose. She realized the boys meant a compliment. The boys often meant a compliment when they were insulting her, so there was no point in being offended. "Look, Sean. Simon. I know you're trying to do something nice—"

"We are not! Nobody's trying to do anything nice!

We're just trying to get out of chores and housework! Cripes, Camille. It's a free movie, what's the big deal?''

Sean sighed, then offered the ultimate sacrifice. "We won't have any farting or burping contests. In fact, we'll do our best not to act normal at all." Then he noticed the dog. "Hey, Darby's looking really good."

"He's been answering to the name Killer for several days now."

"Whatever. Look, you could think of the movie like our chance to thank you for saving Darby's life. Isn't that a good reason? And you like McDonald's, don't you? You don't do that tofu thing like your sister?"

"Oh, man." She could feel her resolve slip a notch. She hadn't considered the one gigantic benefit to leaving home—the chance to escape yet another healthful, herb-laden, vegetable-chocked, leafy dinner. She imagined a French fry. Heaped with salt and ketchup. Then sighed. "Damn. But no. And I really mean no. See, my sister cooks. So I can't just take off when she's already gone to the trouble of making dinner—"

"Oh, she said it was okay. In fact, she called Dad. That was how we knew you could go. She told Dad she was gonna have a makeup party. Or a makeover party. Whatever. Like that. Something for women. And we knew you wouldn't want to have anything to do with that crud, would you, Camille?"

Again, Camille wanted to pinch the bridge of her nose. She didn't give a damn about her appearance. That was the truth. The total truth. But it was starting to grate—just a wee bit—that the boys seemed so sure she didn't care if she were the ugliest female troll to ever walk under a bridge.

She opened her mouth to answer them, yet somehow

at that instant met Pete's eyes. From the distance across the field, it wasn't as if she could really see him, but she felt him looking at her. Felt the flush of warmth from his looking at her...and the flush of memories from the last time she'd ended up in his arms.

"Come on, Cam, come on, come on—"

"All *right*." Their nagging was so relentless that she couldn't think, couldn't keep it together enough to hold firm. And then suddenly the boys were whooping around her, pulling her arms, and then she was boosted into the back of the truck with the pair of them. Killer promptly started a holy howling.

Pete swore, stopped the truck, got out, and lifted the dog into the back of the truck. Camille, openmouthed, watched the dog submit to being carried and then riding in the truck bed as if this were the best thing that had happened to him in a week of Sundays. Pete drove to her backyard and dropped Killer off in the fenced-in area. The dog started the holy howling thing again.

"Quit it. I'm bringing her back in a couple hours," Pete promised the dog.

"I hate to hear him cry. We could have brought him," Sean said.

"To dinner?"

"He could have had a hamburger."

"And then been stuck in the truck for two hours while we watched a movie?"

Sean, having lost that argument, charged into another one. He'd pinned down the horse he wanted. It was a Morgan. Morgans could work or race or do whatever they wanted. Morgans were beautiful. And perfect for the family.

Camille listened to Sean's nagging and Pete's quiet, persistent answers, which saved her having to make any conversation. But she was as aware of Pete as if they were alone. His eyes kept meeting hers in the rearview mirror.

He seemed to be communicating something with his eyes, but she didn't know what. Why had he wanted her to come with him and the boys? And sure, Violet must have called him—otherwise how would he have come up with this harebrained scheme to get her off the farm? But why would he want a woman as goofy and misplaced as she was these days around his two sons?

Naturally, she figured sex was part of the equation. After that last set of kisses, she'd have to be in a coma not to recognize the hormones running amok between them. But it was one thing for her to have a lust attack—she was already bonkers, for heaven's sake. Pete had no motivation in the universe to sleep with a woman who'd turned mean as a rattlesnake and was neurotic besides.

The problem was so confusing that she gave up and sat back. In spite of herself, she almost started to relax. She even started to feel…silly…how stubbornly she'd hermited herself on the farm. No, she didn't want to be about people. She didn't need or want people in her life. Ever again.

But the drive into town was as familiar as her own heartbeat. She'd forgotten how the narrow road twisted around hills, curved into valleys. They passed Firefly Hollow—where every teenager in the county made out. And after that came old man Swisher's pond—there were lots of ponds in the area, but Swisher's had a big old cotton tree with a limb just perfect for swinging into the water.

Pete muttered a swearword when he got jammed up

behind a ponytailed farmer on a tractor—making Camille smile. The farmer was slogging along around fifteen miles an hour and showed no inclination to either budge or get off the road—but then this was Vermont. All the hippies who'd paused here in the '60s never left. Likewise, all the homesteaders who'd come here three hundred years ago—like her family, like Pete's— were just as cussedly independent as their ancestors.

They passed red barns and fences, a hillside that had gotten away from a farmer and was already being taken over by red clover and buttercups. Patches of elms and big old sugar maples shaded parts of the road, and then the landscape suddenly burst into sunshine. Off to the left was the tip of a silvery lake; to the right, a red covered bridge, and then there was one last turn into White Hills.

Her heart unexpectedly lightened. It was going to be fine, she thought. She felt Pete's gaze in the rearview mirror—still talking with Sean about Morgan horses— but checking on her. Or checking in with her.

"You okay?" he mouthed.

As if it was his business. "I think you should get Sean a horse," she said. His son immediately whooped triumphantly, thrilled to have a new ally, and Pete gave her a look that clearly condemned her as a traitor—but it distracted him again.

She didn't want him looking at her. Didn't want to feel that coil of warmth curl up in her belly when he smiled at her, looked at her, tried to *connect* with her.

The town rushed up to grab her attention then, besides. White Hills was named because of the streaks of marble and limestone that looked stark white against the emerald-green countryside. Century-old trees shaded the town. Everything looked exactly as she re-

membered—the tall, skinny brick houses with green
shutters, the white fences smothered in ivy, the cobblestone streets. At the highest point in town was a
white frame church with a sharp white steeple—how
corny could you get? Yet Camille had always loved
that darn church, loved that stereotypical white steeple,
loved the cobblestone streets.

Comforting memories of childhood wrapped her in
a feeling of safety. Unlike everywhere else, White Hills
had never wanted to grow. Apparently they'd been
grudgingly forced to add a McDonald's and a Wal-
Mart, but the Wal-Mart was banished from sight, and
the fast-food places were allowed on Main Street only
if their architecture disguised their nefarious purpose.

"Okay, we've only got twenty minutes before the
movie, so we're just going to do a fast carry-out, all
right with everyone? And no one's getting anything
that's good for them, so don't even try begging me for
vegetables and salads." Pete pulled in, and minutes
later doled out the goodies.

Camille, elbowed between the teenagers, guarded
her French fries and ketchup with her life, and wolfed
down a burger the way she hadn't eaten in months. It
was the town. It was all the childhood memories of
running down Main Street, owning the world, arguing
with her sisters over ice cream, shopping for Christmas
and toys and prom dresses, getting kissed by Billy
Webster in front of Carcutter's Books, getting her dad's
truck stuck in the snow and remembering how she'd
been afraid he'd be mad—but he hadn't been. Everything had seemed possible when she was a kid. Nothing
could really harm her. She not only owned the world;
she grew up believing she could change the world—
even if she *had* thrown up outside Ruby's Hair Salon

when she was fourteen and was positive she'd never live it down.

"You're kidding, right?" Simon said. "You hurled? Right on the street?"

"At rush hour, where everyone in town saw me. I was determined to never show my face for the rest of my life, but a couple days later my mom yanked me out of bed and locked me out of the house and told me to go on to school. My mom was okay with some dramatics. But after a while, enough was enough."

The kids lapped up stories as long as they were either humiliating or gruesome. More surprising to Camille was hearing herself talking at all. Pete parked a couple blocks from the movie theater, which was the closest parking space he could find. So for that short walk, she had the chance to inhale Main Street close up.

Some things had changed, some not. The post office was still located in the General Store, where you could still buy a hoe, a wedding ring and dry powders for headaches—true one-stop shopping. Old Man Riverstern still worked in the window of his silversmithing shop. Adirondack chairs clustered in the porch's shade of the Marble Bridge Café. Most of the lineup had the usual suspects—drugstore, clothing stores, a barber with a red-striped pole. But these days, Camille could see that you could now get your nails done and your behind tattooed…right after you bought food for your horse and ducks at Lamb's Feed Store.

"Damn," Pete muttered. "Don't tell me that's a smile."

"All right. I admit it. Getting away for a couple hours was a good idea." She cocked her head at him.

"But I still feel guilty my sister conned you into dragging me along to a family outing."

"You call going to a movie with two teenagers a family outing? The movie's a comedy. Which means they're going to make rude sounds and laugh themselves half-sick through the entire flick. This is not a treat. This was just a chance to have someone to share the torture."

She heard the strangest sound come out of her mouth. A horse's bray? A baby's chortle. A strangled gasp? Actually, it just seemed to be a plain old laugh. Rusty and husky, but definitely a laugh.

And Pete promptly rewarded her by brushing a kiss on her forehead—she swore he did!—but no one else seemed to see it, and the next instant he was pushing her inside ahead of him and ordering her to get popcorn for four, heaped with butter, get the deal with the double drinks. The boys didn't help her. What teenagers ever volunteered to help? So she got the order, but popcorn spit out of her arms as she tried to juggle it all—helped by both Sean and Simon stealing handfuls and throwing it in the air to catch it.

"And you thought I asked you because of something to do with your sister." Pete came through with the tickets, and grabbed one armload, but when he caught a stranger looking at them, he used his free hand to motion to her. "Those are her children, not mine."

"Hey."

Inside the dark theater, the previews were already running. It wasn't packed—not on a midweek night— but the comedy cast was big-name popular, especially with teenage boys judging from the bulk of the audience. The boys, without asking or needing permission, charged down to the front row.

"I can't sit that close to the front," Pete admitted quietly.

"Neither can I. I can't see, can't hear, can't take the crook in the neck either."

"So just pick your choice of seat and I'll follow behind you."

It was fine, she told herself again. It was embarrassing, how weird she'd become, how nervous she'd been about being in public again. She chose seats up high, where no one was blocking their view. A fat, dripping cola sat between them; their hands were filled with popcorn. Pete's shoulder brushed hers and she could smell the soap he used, his skin, feel the nearness of him like a voltage charge in her pulse. But it was okay.

She was so sure.

And it was. For ten minutes. Maybe even fifteen.

There was no single moment when that changed. Nothing specific to mark the instant when everything started going wrong. The comedy was the usual—an urban slapstick, a pair of cops without a brain between them, tripping over criminals and apologizing, arresting the innocent, that whole yadda yadda. Almost everyone in the audience got caught in some outright belly laughs. So did she.

Or she thought she was laughing. It was just...she suddenly realized how dark the theater was. Pitch-dark. And one of the movie scenes started out on a quiet suburban street, with rain glistening on trees and making diamonds of the streetlights.

Just like that night.

Exactly like that night when she'd been walking home in her high heels with Robert. Her feet ached and she'd had too much wine but she was still laughing,

laughing, high on marriage and Robert and life and her job and herself.

Camille blinked, willing herself to concentrate on the movie, only suddenly the darkness wasn't friendly but whispering with a thousand menacing shadows. Evil. How could anyone know where it was coming from? She'd seen the three young men walking toward them quite clearly, but it didn't mean anything. They were on a city street; lots of people walked around at all hours. But that night, of course, it did mean something. She saw a glimpse of ugliness in the one boy's eyes— she *saw*, and in that instant realized that she was trapped in a living nightmare. It happened so fast it was all too late, all too late, all too late. Her pulse slammed with panic; her whole body flushed in a cold sweat.

"Cam? Camille, what's wrong?"

She sensed Pete turning toward her, heard his immediate calming whisper, but the memories were firing at her like machine guns. She summoned the most normal voice she could. "Nothing, Pete. I just need to get up for a minute."

Actually, she needed to get completely out of there. Now. Yesterday. Sooner than yesterday. She crawled over Pete and bolted toward the stairs. She couldn't catch her breath, as if all the air were trapped in her lungs. She heard her heart hammering desperately in her ears, tasted the sick nausea of fear, felt a choking sensation in her throat. She tripped, almost fell on the last stair, and then hurtled on, down the aisle, then into the sudden harsh artificial light, down that hall, then through the heavy metal doors and finally out, out, into the fresh night air.

Only then did she realize that Pete was right behind her.

Six

The instant Pete realized she was upset, he took off after her, but it wasn't that easy to catch up. She charged out of the dark theater so fast that he wasn't positive which direction she'd gone. The rest rooms were tucked off to the left. The main lobby led to exit doors off to the right. And straight ahead was a long hall leading to other movies being shown and then a back exit.

Pete jogged forward, then spun back. Midshow, the lobbies and halls were library-quiet, so when he heard the crack of a metal door at the end of the far hall, he immediately keeled around, guessing it had to be Cam. He caught a glimpse of red—the shoulder of her red long-sleeved T-shirt—just before the door closed again.

Guilt clogged his throat. Not a little guilt. A whole steam shovelful. Maybe he'd never been the ultrasensitive type of guy, but he wasn't usually this bad a jerk.

How could he have done this to her? What was he *thinking?*

His palm slapped the back door open—which made his hand hurt like hell, but didn't assuage the guilt worth beans.

And there she was.

The theater's back door led to nothing but a parking lot and some scruffy woods. The sun was a red ball, hiding in those leafy trees, dropping fast now. The real world was only a block away—he could hear traffic sounds, even distant voices—but here, there was literally nothing and no one. A chill sneaked behind the evening sunshine, putting a brisk bite in the air.

And Camille had sunk down on the cement curb, arms wrapped around her knees, just kind of rocking herself with her eyes squeezed closed. She never opened her eyes or looked back, yet before he said a single word, she piped up, "Pete, I'm fine. Go back inside with the boys. I'll come back in. I just needed some air."

Okay. So Camille had easily guessed that he'd follow her—but he should have easily guessed how the movie was likely to affect her. The kids had pushed for going, said it was a comedy. But he hadn't asked a single question—or he'd have known it was going to be about cops and city crime.

"Go back in," she repeated, and motioned him with her hand, sounding aggravated now.

He came closer instead. In a split second—faster than a second—he realized he'd fallen so deep and so hard in love with her that he couldn't think straight.

Of course he'd realized he was increasingly miserable around her—but not that he was hooked this hard. It was the look of her. That stupid, butchered, chopped off hair—but damn, it framed her face pixie-fashion, made her soft brown eyes look huge. Right now those eyes held an ocean of pain and her skin was whiter than chalk. Her hands were clenched in a clear effort to control their shaking, and her frail shoulders were hunched, making her look more fragile, more beaten—and it killed him. Frustrated him. Enraged him. Too see his Camille this over her head, this whipped by anything.

"You're having an anxiety attack."

"Yup. If you've never seen one before, don't get your liver in an uproar. I do this a few times a week. Just to keep in practice. It'll pass in a minute."

Her effort to treat it lightly made him sick. He hunkered down on the cement stoop next to her. "This one was brought on by the movie?"

"Who knows. Anything can set one off. I hear a strange sound—even if it'd be an innocuous sound to anybody else—and *shazam*, just like that, I'm suddenly sweating and acting like a complete idiot. It's really annoying. Would you just go back inside? Please. It's embarrassing enough to be such a wuss without having someone else see it. And it'll pass. In fact, it'll pass faster if you leave me alone. Other people can't help. It just takes me a few minutes of concentration to pull myself together."

He wanted to pull her in his arms so bad he could taste it, but some internal instinct stopped him. He'd pulled her into his arms before. It hadn't brought them closer together; it seemed to make her even warier. Camille treated concern as if it were a poison she could choke on. Still, he wanted—needed—to understand more of what she was dealing with. "The movie. I didn't realize. I thought it was just a comedy—"

"I know. Don't waste guilt on me, Pete. You didn't do anything wrong. I knew better than to come into town."

"Well, that sounds pretty unfair. Unless you were planning on staying home forever?"

"No, of course not. I need to make a living. Have to find work again. And I will. I just need a little more time to get past this." Her head shot up. "Do me a favor and *don't* suggest going to a shrink."

"I wasn't going to." He might not be brilliant with women, but Pete knew when to shut up or risk being strangled.

"I don't need any damn shrink to tell me I'm acting like an idiot. Or why. I'm not stupid."

"Did I say you were?" Oh, man. That belligerent chin. That fierce well of pain in her eyes. That soft skin. A mantra kept whispering through his mind with the same old refrain: *Let me love you. Let me help you. Let me protect you and make sure no one ever hurts you again.* But of course he couldn't make those promises—he didn't have the power. Or the right.

"I can handle my own life, Pete. Just because I'm having trouble doesn't mean I'm incapable of fixing it."

Sheesh. Somehow she seemed to feel he was attacking her—which he wasn't, and he wanted to correct that impression, except that the show of belligerence seemed to be doing her good. Fresh color bloomed in her cheeks. Her hands had stopped shaking. And she was still talking.

"There's a reason I'm taking so long to get my life back together. It's about power."

"Power," he echoed, wanting to encourage her even if she wasn't making a lick of sense.

She nodded. "Both my parents raised me to believe that I was powerful. Seriously. I grew up believing that I had power over my life, over what I could become, over what I could do. Most people complain about feeling insecure all the time. Not me. I wasn't raised insecure, I was raised to believe I could conquer the world—if I just worked hard and kept my nose clean and stood up for the things that mattered."

He hung his arms over his knees. "That sounds exactly like how I'm trying to raise my sons."

"Well, don't. Because then when something happens, like when I was attacked, it's like a double blow. I'd never felt helpless before. I'd never felt…impotent. It was as if those three men took it all away. Not just Robert, not just life as I knew it, but me. They took away *me*."

Again he wanted nothing more than to pull her in his arms, to love her. To shield her. The urge was so strong he almost couldn't suck it back…. But damnation, this wasn't about him, and what he wanted to do. It was about her. About Camille believing she'd lost herself. And about a woman who spit back sympathy if you dared try to give it to her.

"So you're just planning on hiding out on the farm rather than risk being any part of real life?" he asked.

"Pardon?" She turned to him with a flash of vulnerability in her eyes.

"That's what you're saying, isn't it? That even going to a movie is too much for you to handle."

Her jaw almost dropped. "I can handle it—"

"Well, you're out here shaking. I'd hardly call that 'handling it.'" He saw the shocked look in her eyes, the sting of hurt. And pushed harder. "If you weren't

Play the Lucky Hearts Game

and get...

2 FREE BOOKS

and a **FREE MYSTERY GIFT...**

yes! **YOURS to KEEP!**

I have scratched off the silver card. Please send me my *2 FREE BOOKS* and *FREE mystery GIFT*. I understand that I am under no obligation to purchase any books as explained on the back of this card.

Scratch Here!

then look below to see what your cards get you... 2 Free Books & a Free Mystery Gift!

▲ DETACH AND MAIL CARD TODAY! ▲

326 SDL DU6S   225 SDL DU69

FIRST NAME   LAST NAME

ADDRESS

APT.#   CITY

STATE/PROV.   ZIP/POSTAL CODE

(S-D-08/03)

Twenty-one gets you
2 FREE BOOKS
and a **FREE MYSTERY GIFT!**

Twenty gets you
2 FREE BOOKS!

Nineteen gets you
1 FREE BOOK!

TRY AGAIN!

feeling so sorry for yourself, you'd be going back in the movie, proving it was no big deal."

More hurt. But those shoulders stiffened like soldiers. "It *isn't* any big deal. I'm going back in the movie right this minute. I told you. I just needed a few seconds to get some air." She bolted to her feet. "And just because you caught me with my hands shaking for a second doesn't mean I'm some needy little wimp. It happens. I admit that. But it's happening tons less than it did. I'm perfectly fine."

"So you say."

"You're damn right, so I say."

She stomped to the door, discovered—no surprise—that the back exit door was locked from the outside, and then stomped all the way around the theater, into the lobby, and back into the darkened movie to the exact same seats they'd had before. She didn't speak to him through the rest of the movie. Or during the drive home either.

The boys never sensed anything was wrong. The whole ride, they never quit talking, replaying every scene and chortling over the good parts the way they always did after a movie. As Pete drove, he realized he hadn't seen how the boys related to Camille before.

He'd sensed that his sons had somehow accepted her, which was pretty darn astounding, since they hadn't had a positive word to say about a woman since their mother took off. It was both fascinating and unnerving to see how different they were with Camille— partly, it seemed, because she made no attempt to mother them or correct them or "play adult" with them in any sense.

He noted their behavior with Cam. Noted *her* behavior with them. But mostly he noticed that the air between the adults could have frozen ice cubes in a rain forest.

He'd hurt her. She hadn't expected him to say anything mean or critical. And implying she couldn't handle something always had been, likely always would be, like waving a red flag in front of a bull. At the time, he hadn't seen any other choice. He'd been trying to find a way to get to her. But Cam had put up so many fierce defenses that getting to her by any conventional means simply didn't work.

In her driveway, his headlights flashed on the snow fence she'd set up for Darby, who promptly began an exuberant symphony of snarling and barking the instant the truck pulled up. Camille pushed out of the seat and vaulted down with a good-night for the boys, but noticeably no comment for him.

He'd hurt her, all right. Only it felt as if it were his own heart that had been stabbed.

As soon as the truck lights disappeared, Camille hustled in the cottage, rooted high and low until she came across the dog leash, and then hustled outside again.

Killer was still howling and snarling himself into a frenzy. "Shut up, you witless dolt. There's no one here but me. C'mere."

The dog, naturally, hated the leash. "I know. I haven't been making you use the leash anymore, but this is different. The fact is, I can't trust you. I'm willing to take you for a walk to run off that energy, but I can't risk your running off and attacking someone. Believe me, I understand your bad temper. I'm in exactly the same kind of mood. But right now, you only have two choices—a walk with the leash, or no walk."

It was hard enough to clip on the leash when the dog

wasn't being rambunctious and ornery, but tonight it was dark besides. Finally she managed, but right as she was pushing to her feet, the dog licked her cheek.

"I don't love you, so don't be thinking I care," Camille scolded, but Killer seemed as unimpressed with this threat as all her others. Once she unlatched the gate, he bounded beside her, ears perked high and alert, walking to her exact pace.

The long night walks had become a pattern. She'd been sleeping better ever since she'd begun working in the lavender—the backbreaking work guaranteed she'd fall asleep. But sometimes the ridiculous nightmares still plagued her, and then walking seemed to help. Stumbling in the dark wasn't ideal, but Killer was sure-footed, and the farm path around the acres of lavender had become a familiar route.

Since no one was around, she talked to the dog. It seemed a little saner than talking to herself. And it didn't seem to matter what she said or how mean she said it, Killer seemed to listen. In fact, the damn dog seemed to crave the sound of her voice—not that she did it for his sake.

Tonight, though, she set up a fast hiking pace and didn't talk at all. Killer, tuned to her channel, hiked and watched—with only a few breaks to tear off into the bushes and lift a leg.

The brisk walk helped Camille work up a fume. The nerve of that man! Implying she couldn't handle a movie if she wanted to! Implying she was a coward for not leaving the farm!

Pete hadn't been through what she had, for God's sake. And for the first time in all these weeks, she'd actually been trying to tell him. Not a lot. But she hadn't opened up at all since the whole thing happened, and she thought she could trust Pete. Instead, he'd implied that she couldn't handle even something so little as going to a movie.

It chafed like a rug burn.

Not hurt. Camille had no intention of ever allowing her feelings so out of control that being hurt was even a possibility. But she could be…chafed. And aggravated. And insulted.

The whole damn world had been nice to her since the attack. Everyone had appreciated what a terrible and unbearable thing she'd been through. *Everyone.* And there she'd shared the tiniest bit with Pete, and he'd made out like she was a wimp. She was inclined to…why, she was inclined to…

She promptly stumbled on a rock and nearly tripped. Not because she was clumsy, but because she glanced up and saw Pete standing on her back porch. He stood directly under the porch light, as if knowing she'd tend to be afraid of anyone showing up after dark, yet she felt no fear. If she felt a shiver seep into her pulse, it was caused from something far different from fear. Although her first thought was just: Good, now she'd have the chance to punch his lights out.

Killer, of course, started immediately barking—and because Camille wasn't prepared, the dog yanked the leash from her hand and tore off toward Pete, sounding like a canine version of Sylvester Stallone on a Rambo rampage.

"Oh, shut up, Darby," Pete said.

The dog promptly sat down and then lay down, tongue lolling. Camille shook her head, flabbergasted at the dog's docility, but Killer couldn't hold her attention for long. Her gaze glued on Pete and wouldn't let go. "What are you doing here?"

"Waiting for you."

"Obviously. I meant why."

"Because I believed what you said. That you're fine. And I had the impression you were sick and tired of people treating you as if you were going to break."

"I am," she admitted. "Tired to bits of people tiptoeing around me, treating me like fluff."

"Well, you can take it to the bank, Cam. I won't be one of those treating you like fluff. I think you can take anything I can dish out."

"You're damn right I can," she assured him.

"Good," he murmured, and reached for her.

She never saw the kiss coming. Never had a clue that was where he was leading. She felt a long, slow *woooosh* inside her when his mouth came down on hers, in a kiss that started hard and deep and just kept coming.

His tongue was inside her mouth before she'd scrabbled a spare ounce of oxygen. The screen door clapped behind them; his palm slapped down the porch light switch—and that was the last instant his hands were anywhere but on her.

The cottage was devil-black for an instant…but not really. Moonlight silvered through the naked windows. The light was perfect for kisses so naked they cut right past courtesies and politeness and pretenses.

Camille scrambled to make sense of a world that had become a storm of sensation, electric thunder, instant lightning. His tongue was making love with her tongue. His mouth, wet and hot, was molding hers. His hands, palms splayed, slid down her sides, inch by inch in a claim of ownership. She heard what his hands were saying as if they could talk: *I own you. Maybe not tomorrow, maybe not next year, but right now, babe, that body of yours is all mine.*

Her first sip of champagne had never made her this high, this dizzy. She simply didn't do this.

She did nice sex.

She and Robert had always had nice sex. They'd shared cute little private jokes. They'd been comfortable, careful with each other. They'd learned all the things new lovers learn.

This wasn't comfortable. This was scary and wild. This was turning on a faucet full force. "Pete—"

"I've got protection."

"That's not what I was going to say."

"If you want to say no, then say it. Anything else, we can talk about later."

She opened her mouth, planning to say no. Planning to insist he slow down until she found her mind again—the one he was turning into shambles from the inside out. But instead of saying no, for a completely unknown reason, she lifted up on tiptoe and wrapped her arms around his neck.

If she'd been looking for trouble, she found it—faster than a sting, hotter than a fire. In flashes she saw the moonlight on his harsh face, his soft eyes. He peeled her shirt over her head. She peeled his shirt over his. Maybe for a tornado they could have stopped. Maybe.

He swore, twice, just trying to get her into the bedroom. Packing boxes still hadn't been put away. Some obstacle connected with his shin, another with his foot. Moonlight didn't extend to the shadows and doorways…but his kisses did. His touch did.

Pete seemed to know all the private places she'd been hiding in the dark.

Somewhere near the foot of the bed, he peeled the bra straps down her arms, then trailed the straps with his mouth, laving, biting, then baring her breasts for his view. He looked and kept looking, even as he was slowly zipping down her jeans and pushing them off her. There was naked and then there was *naked*. She'd been naked with Robert, but somehow she'd never felt this completely…exposed.

She kept telling herself that she was afraid, not ready, that she wanted to stop. But his hands were in her hair, and those kisses kept coming. She wasn't protesting. She was claiming all the kisses he offered, taking everything he gave, demanding more, inviting more. When he lowered her to the bed, the old mattress springs creaked and groaned, not used to the weight of two wildly impatient lovers. The sheets felt moonchilled, where her skin was unbearably hot. Fevered.

She hadn't felt anything but anger in so long. She couldn't explain what was happening. Morality didn't seem to matter. This couldn't be love…but it did seem to be about trusting Pete. Or his forcing her to trust him, because he gave and gave and gave. Liquid kisses. Golden kisses. Intimate kisses that tracked from her ankle to the inside of her thigh to the heart of her.

Need spiraled through her body, exploded through her senses, a fierce, urgent hunger that had nothing to do with lust—and yet everything to do with it. Desire coiled in her tighter than a spring, ready to let loose when he suddenly laughed, a low sound of masculine delight…and then he blew a raspberry in her navel to make her laugh, too. Laughter and sex, who'd have thought they went together? But when he nuzzled her breasts, her breath started coming in short, harsh gasps. As sweet as the laughter had been, suddenly she was in a desperate hurry for him, inside her, *now*.

She'd been torn apart for so many months. Alone for so many months. She didn't know how to put her life back together. Wasn't sure if she had a life that could be mended anymore.

But right then, it was as if Pete were taking her to some other place…a place where nothing existed but this urgent excitement. This rush of sensation. His wild mouth, his wicked eyes. His misbehaving hands, coaxing her to do things she didn't do, to think things she didn't think, to behave like a woman different than Camille. She was his lover. His abandoned, earthy lover at that moment, no one else, nothing else.

He pulled her beneath him, rising up, giving her a breath's space—but she saw the glaze of desire in his eyes, saw the sheen of control in his face. She met his first thrust with her legs tight around him, then raised them higher and tighter yet, as if she could take him in as deep as her soul. He whispered something about how sweet she was, how wet, how tight, just for him, but he was already building a rhythm, pumping a beat, taking her on a long, fast ride.

She felt her spine arching, felt her pulse rushing and gathering speed, heard the call from her throat with his name on it. What she'd been so sure was lust wasn't lust at all, but somehow magic. She felt protected in the circle of his arms, in his heat, in his warmth. He was stronger than she was and until those moments, that instant, she hadn't known how strong she'd been. Or how badly she'd needed to let go, for a few minutes, to just be…weak. To be herself. To not hold up those steel emotional walls for just a little while.

And then release came to her like a sweet rush of

rain, cleansing, healing, freeing. One burst of pleasure
followed another, until she lay in his arms, breathless,
whipped. He scooped her up and just held her. She
heard his thundering heartbeat under her ear, felt his
hand stroking down her shoulder and spine.

Gradually she became aware that clouds had chased
across the moon. The room was darker, a night chill
sneaking in. She'd felt the helpless smile on her lips,
yet now felt that smile dying as her eyes opened.

There was no sudden sting of reality. The feeling of
being cradled against his brawny chest was wonderful,
the sensation of being sexually and emotionally sated
was a call of life and hope that she hadn't felt in
months...if ever in her life. Yet when she suddenly
lifted her head, she saw Pete's eyes in the darkness,
watching, waiting, as if he'd been half-tense in antici-
pation of her coming awake again.

"Thank you," she whispered.

"Don't steal my lines. And I can't talk quite yet. I
don't know what just happened, but it feels like something on a par with hang gliding off Mt. Everest."

A small smile. "Did we wear you out?"

"We? You did it all. And damn, you're so small.
Where you've been hiding all that power and passion,
stranger?" Still his hand stroked, stroked, as if he were
gentling a kitten who was braced to flee. "I knew we'd
be good. It had to be good, Cam. But I never thought
it'd be like this."

"Neither did I." But his warmth, his words of praise
and tenderness, aroused an uneasy thread in her pulse.
"I haven't felt alive in months. I didn't know I could
feel...anything. Much less anything like this."

"There's no way you could have healed fast. You
had a terrible hurt."

Another uneasy thread bucked in her pulse. She touched his jaw, pushed back an unruly shock of hair from his brow. Whatever this had been about, she didn't regret it. Couldn't. He'd made her feel alive the way she never had, never thought she could.

But everything wasn't about her. Pete had two sons—two vulnerable boys whose mom had left them, who didn't trust women. He couldn't just take any woman in his life. And Camille couldn't imagine a woman less suited to be a healthy, trustworthy role model for his kids—or even be good for him. She barely knew what she was doing one day to the next.

"What are we going to call this, MacDougal?" she asked softly.

"How about if we don't call it anything? I don't need labels."

She swallowed. "I don't like labels either. But I don't want to hurt you."

"I'm a big boy."

"I noticed that."

He tapped the tip of her nose. "*That* wasn't what I meant."

"Oh. Well. What I meant was...I don't know where we go from here."

"We go wherever you want. Whatever feels natural."

A pile of horse hockey if ever she'd heard one. Camille knew about vulnerability. Sometimes she felt so fragile she knew she could shatter if the wind blew from the wrong direction. And Pete looked tough and strong and mighty, because he was. But he hadn't been a few minutes ago, in her arms. He'd needed her, no different than she'd needed him.

"I'm okay with doing what feels natural," she said

softly, "as long as neither of us build up unreasonable expectations."

He stilled. His eyes met hers, unbending even in the darkness. "What are you worried about, Cam? Spill it out."

She was worried about needing him too much. About hurting someone who'd been impossibly good to her. About failing a man who deserved someone who would never fail him. So she said, "I won't lie to you, MacDougal. I loved Robert. I still love Robert. I don't have the power to make those feelings go away."

"No one's asking you to," he said sharply, but then he pulled her in his arms for a second time. The first kiss insured she was cut off from saying anything more. And then he made love to her, insuring she didn't have the energy for anything but him—and them.

She woke once in the night, on the tip of a nightmare, but she found herself soothed and smoothed in Pete's arms, and the bad dream just seemed to disappear.

The next time she opened her eyes, it was daybreak. And he was gone.

Seven

For three days in a row, the family had complained that Pete was as much fun to be around as a crabby porcupine. So this morning, the instant he heard sounds of life stirring upstairs, he sucked down a mug of coffee and pasted on a stupid, happy smile. By the time vigorous fighting had broken out between the twins, he had the eggs whipped to a frenzy. By the time he heard the sound of his father's cane on the stairs, he popped down the toast.

His dad showed up in the doorway first, shooting him a wary glance. "Gonna be a hot one, they say," Ian claimed as he ambled into the kitchen. "Pretty rare to have eighty degrees in May."

"Uh-huh." When Pete heard the grumpiness in his tone, he deliberately repeated, "Uh-huh," with more boisterous enthusiasm.

His father squinted at him in surprise, then poured a

mug and settled across the counter. When Pete offered no further conversation, Ian ventured, "You get some sleep last night? Seems like I heard you pacing around for three nights in a row, figured you weren't feeling well."

"Couldn't be better," Pete said heartily. "How're doing this morning, Dad?"

That shocked Ian into complete silence. Pete never asked about Ian's state of health—not because he didn't love his father—but because Ian generally answered in minute detail about every ache and pain. Ian liked being coddled, where Pete didn't believe it was good for him. This morning, though, his father didn't answer his health question, only watched Pete serve him eggs and toast and juice.

"You're waiting on me," Ian said, in the same disbelieving tone he'd use to announce Elvis hunkering down at their kitchen table.

"Just thought we should all start the day with a good breakfast."

"I'm not complaining," Ian said hastily, and taking advantage of his son being pleasant, tried a new line of conversation. "I couldn't help but notice the special deliveries you got yesterday. Looked like some thick envelopes. New work?"

"Yeah." And normally, the arrival of new work would have revved his personal jets. He did all kinds of translating projects, but the scientific translating work he did for Langley was his favorite, always fascinating and different, always something new to spin his mind around. Right now, though, there was only one thing he wanted the skill to translate—and that wasn't scientific developments, but Camille. No amount of replaying what she said seemed to help him analyze what she really meant—or what she really wanted.

The boys clattered downstairs. Eggs got shoveled onto plates. Ian punched on CNBC. Sun poured in the east windows.

When Pete looked out, though, he didn't see the sun-lit grass or the dewy glisten in his apple orchards. He saw her. His mind's view whispered back three nights. He saw Cam's face by moonlight, the magic in her eyes, her silky white naked skin. The way she'd come alive for him. Apart for him. Gone wild for him, with him.

For damn sure, he hadn't been hurt that she'd ended the night with honesty. Her confession that she was still in love with her dead husband came as absolutely no surprise. She'd never given him a reason to expect any-thing else. A man would have to be an idiot to not realize the tragedy was still haunting her. Camille was nothing like Debbie. When Cam loved, she *loved*. Ob-viously, she'd never be having such a hard time getting over Robert's death if she hadn't loved him so damn much.

A glass of juice spilled. Ian babbled on about an eye doctor appointment. The boys only had a couple weeks of school left, and they had plans. "I'm not going to bug you about a horse again, Dad. I'm just saying…."

"It's okay," he said.

"You mean, it's okay that I can get a horse this summer?"

He leaned forward, bracing his elbows on the counter, looking out. He'd never made love with her because he expected any kind of return. The chemistry was explosive, so yeah, there was plenty of selfishness on his part. He wasn't trying to claim that he'd made love for her sake. But that really wasn't the whole picture. He hated seeing her shut herself off from life. He also didn't want her getting her feet wet with some guy who'd hurt her—something he knew he'd never do. He wanted to be the one who helped her heal. What was wrong with that?

Nothing. Absolutely nothing.

Making love hadn't hurt her. Hadn't hurt him. Her admitting she was still hung up on Robert was an honest, honorable thing to tell him.

He was happy she had.

Very happy.

A yellow school bus suddenly braked at the end of the driveway. The back door slammed once, then twice, as the boys pelted outside.

"I think Simon broke the remote control. Didn't want to tell you, but from the looks of the situation, I believe it found its way into the bathtub."

"Sure," Pete said.

Ian brought the breakfast dishes to the sink. That was the closest he ever came to doing dishes directly. "I can't believe you agreed to buy that boy a horse. Ask me, it's proof you've completely lost your mind. But if you're up for a horse, I might as well buy Simon and Sean a truck of their own. That okay with you?"

"Sure."

"Maybe I'll take them on a trip to Alaska next week, too."

"Okay."

"Are you going to be in the office this morning or out in the orchards or what? Where are you going to be?"

Pete shook himself awake, stirred from the window. "I'll be working in the back office for at least an hour.

But then I'm going to pick up a few truckloads of mulch and round up a crew.''

''Ah. For Camille's lavender.'' His dad almost choked on a guffaw, the sound so unexpected that Pete pivoted around and looked at him in surprise.

''What's so funny?''

''I just think it's pretty amazing. I could tell you the sun turned blue, and you'd never hear the conversation, but if I mention anything related to Camille, you're all ears.''

''I don't know what you're talking about.''

''Just because I've gotten old doesn't mean I've lost all memory of what a young buck feels like. Tuesday was the first time you were gone all night since the divorce. I was pretty sure you weren't playing dominoes.''

Pete opened his mouth to deny his dad's assumption—off the cuff, he didn't have a clear-cut lie on mind, only the intention to come through with a good one. Only his dad—the one who'd been trying to make the family believe he needed help to walk across a room—skedaddled from sight. In fact, he trundled in the other room so fast that Pete had no chance to think up any kind of good lie. For his dad.

Or for himself.

Camille saw the cars parked outside the Herb Haven, but she still trounced inside. For three days, she'd let herself stew and fester instead of confronting her sister. Naturally, she wouldn't say anything directly in front of customers, but it was time to corner Violet and have it out.

She spotted Violet right away and motioned to let her know she was there, then just wandered up and down aisles, staying out of the way. Her sister was waiting on a guy. Camille could hear the man talking—he was apparently looking for a present for his wife. A girl present. Something that cost around fifty bucks and smelled good and that his wife would like—those factors seemed to sum up his entire descriptive criteria.

"Don't you worry about a thing, Jacob. I'll fix you up." Violet was wearing another one of her big, sappy hats—heaven knew why. She was also wearing lace-up shoes with heels, a vintage lace blouse, and earrings that hung to her shoulders.

Camille wouldn't have worn the outfit in a coffin, but for a brief moment she felt like something a cat dragged in from the rain. It wasn't that long ago that she'd loved her sassy business suits and spent a shameless fortune on shoes and jewelry. She'd always tended toward tailored pieces, sterling collars and single bangles, none of the froufrou and beads that Vi loved, but she'd never been unkempt or uncaring about her appearance, the way she was now. She caught a glimpse of her wind-burned cheeks and wildly tossed hair in a mirror and unconsciously touched her face, thinking of Pete—before swiftly turning away.

Violet seemed to know this Jacob. Camille thought she might know him herself—his voice and name sounded familiar, as if they might have gone to school together. Distracted, she watched her sister in action. Violet kept fussing over the guy until his face turned beet red, bemusing Camille. Vi was so completely different around certain people. She was smart. Maybe she was a little eccentric in a couple of minor ways, but she'd always had a big IQ. Around certain males, though, Vi seemed to talk in blond and behave in ways that deliberately scared men from having a normal conversation.

By the time Jacob left, Camille was so puzzled by her sister's behavior that she almost forgot she was foot-tapping upset with her. Unfortunately, the shop was busy. After Jacob left, a plump grandma bought chamomile tea and evening primrose oil. Then a pair of women walked in. Finally, the store was quiet for a few minutes.

"Hey," Vi started to say.

"You traitor. You sicced Pete on me. How could you?"

"Huh?"

"Three nights ago. When I said I was staying home. You threatened me that if I didn't get off the farm, you were going to do something. But I thought you meant that you were going to do something ugly—like call Mom."

"Why would I call Mom and worry her?"

"Well, that's why I thought you wouldn't! But then I thought you'd call Daisy."

Violet slid behind the counter, where she'd obviously been creating dried herb and flower arrangements until the flood of customers. The counter was mounded with heaps of leaves and fronds and smelly stuff. "Actually, I did call Daisy."

Camille's jaw dropped. "You tattletaled on me to Daisy?"

"Uh-huh. Reach behind you on that top shelf for the spools of ribbons, okay? I need the gold and red and, hmm, maybe the pale orchid. And yes, I tattletaled to Daisy. We must have talked about twenty minutes, brainstorming ways to push you into going out in public again."

"I would have gone into town when I was ready!"

"Maybe," Violet conceded. "But the point is, this way worked. You went to town. I knew Pete could get you to do it. And I also thought it was probably a good idea for him besides—hand me the emerald ribbon, too, okay? And here. Cut it in foot-long strips...."

"I'm not here to cut your damned ribbon." Camille grabbed the scissors. "What'd you mean about it being good for Pete?"

"You know." Stems and leaves and sticks flew every which way. "Pete hasn't been the same since the divorce. You know how he was in high school—Mr. Bad Boy. Always full of the devil, full of fun. He was never mean—not that kind of devil—but he loved to play, loved to party, had a little wild streak. He could charm a teacher out of giving a test. Skip school and not get in trouble—"

"Could you cut to the chase? I was in school with you guys, remember?"

"Well, he met Debbie in college. In the beginning they seemed real tuned. She was real gregarious, a life-of-the-party type. And I guess they were fine when they were first married. At least that's how I heard it. But then they had the twins, and a year after that his mom died." Violet shook her head. "Big life things, you know? Only it's as if Pete grew up and she never did."

"What do you mean?"

"Have you got my ribbons cut?"

Sheesh. It was like blackmail. Having to listen to all this extra chat and work, too. But she had to hand over the cut ribbons before Violet was willing to continue.

"Those babies...from the day the boys were born, Pete was just crazy for them. Everybody noticed. He was the one walking the floor at night, taking them to the pediatrician for their shots, taking them for walks, the whole shebang. As far as I know, Debbie wanted a baby, at least in theory, but maybe she didn't realize how tied down she was going to be. And having twins made it worse."

"How come I never heard any of this before?" Camille said impatiently.

"Everyone knew."

"I didn't."

Violet took the mess of weeds and ribbon and some paper, and somehow, when she stuck it all in a vase, it looked like a zillion dollar florist arrangement...talking the whole time. "Cam, you were in college, and then you got that great marketing job, and then you were with Robert. You weren't thinking about the stuff going on back home. Neither was I—when I was with Simpson. Anyway. It wasn't just that Pete settled down after the boys were born. He also came back to White Hills because his dad needed help after his mother died. Debbie went nuts. Whining all the time about country life, nothing to do. Initially I'm not sure if Pete ever intended to stay here. It was more temporary, to help his dad."

"But—?" Prodding Violet to get to the bottom line was like waiting for Congress to balance the budget.

"But he liked the land. And the boys just loved it here. And then he got into that other work—I don't know what he does exactly, except that it's something he can do at home. And that was the point, that he could make a good living and yet still be available for his kids—because by that time, Debbie sure wasn't much of a mother."

They both glanced up when the door opened, but it was just Killer pushing his nose in, looking for Camille. Three cats promptly leaped to tall shelves. Violet said quietly, "I think Pete really knew she was playing around quite a while before she took off."

Camille ignored Killer, ignored the cats, ignored the ribbons. She blurted out, "I just can't believe any woman would play around on Pete."

"Neither can I." Violet finished another breathtakingly artistic arrangement. Of course, she left enough of a mess to fill a trash truck, but neither woman was paying attention by then, anyway. "It's not as if Pete and I ever clicked. We didn't. But I still always thought he was a hunk. Not just because he's good-looking, you know? But because some guys just come across as…"

"Male with a capital *M*," Camille supplied.

"Yeah, exactly. You can just look and know some guys will be good lovers, some won't. It's in their eyes. It's in how they move. You can just tell they like sex—"

"Um, Vi. All men like sex. They come out of the womb reaching for a boob."

Violet grinned. "Well, I know that. But I meant… some men like the pleasure of it, the touching, all of it, not just the getting-off part." She paused. "That's theory, of course. Everything I learned wrong about sex, I learned from Simpson. Anyway—"

"Anyway," Camille echoed.

"The point is, Pete seemed to lose all his spirit after Debbie left. He turned into a complete Sobersides. I don't mean there's anything to criticize. Cripes, he's a football dad, Boy Scout leader, volunteer for anything in the community involving kids. But ask him to a party, and he's got a dozen excuses why he can't go. And they say in town that he never goes out, no matter what woman's tried chasing him. He's just seemed to lose his pizzazz, you know?''

No, she hadn't known.

But as she trudged back home, she felt more troubled than ever that they'd made love. It was one thing for her to do something insane in a moment of impulse—and wild chemistry—but another for her to risk hurting someone else. Violet had made her see Pete as far more vulnerable than showed on the surface. For damn sure, he didn't need a woman in his life who he couldn't trust, not after what his ex-wife had put him through.

She was within yards of the cottage when she heard the unexpected roar of engines. Killer paid no attention. The dog was used to the sound of trucks and tractors. And so was Camille—but not coming from anyone on Campbell land, much less from the direction of the lavender field.

She hustled to the top of the knoll, where she tried to sort out the commotion. Pete's white truck glinted in the sun on the far side of the field. Strangers were milling all over the place. Three truckloads of mulch were being dumped up and down the rows of lavender, and then tractors with blades were pushing the mulch closer to the plants, with workers pitchforking it directly under the plants from there.

Her jaw didn't drop in complete shock—because she already knew Pete was capable of massive interfering. But knowing that he was a hopelessly take-charge kind of guy and realizing he'd become even more embroiled in helping her were two different things. She hurled down the hill with her scowl and her vicious dog, practicing dire threats under her breath until she could catch up to deliver them in person.

Initially his back was to her—he was speaking Spanish to a man in a plaid shirt who obviously worked for Pete. When the small man noticed her, he gestured quickly, which was all it took for Pete to spin around.

"Hi, Cam...Camille, this is big Al. He's been my farm foreman for a bunch of years. And Al, this is Camille Campbell."

"Nice to meet you, Al." She shook his hand, then whipped around to Pete. "MacDougal, I want a word with you."

"Sure, I—"

"*Now.*" She—and Killer—did their best to herd him behind the shade of the giant maple tree, because it just didn't seem politically correct to murder a man in front of people who worked for him. But she was doubly tempted to do bodily harm when Pete smiled at her.

He knew perfectly well she was susceptible to his smiles. He knew perfectly well what they'd done the last time he'd smiled at her like that. He couldn't be glad to see her. No one was glad to see an ornery curmudgeon with a chronic case of PMS who was neurotic to the nth degree. He also didn't find her attractive. No man could find a woman attractive who'd abandoned nail files and lipstick and grooming and was wearing clothes so big they'd smother a shroud.

She was already worried about him, and now that smile of his worried her even more. What if her hermit-type insanity was infectious? What kind of influence could she be on him or for him if he started behaving as sick and demented as she was?

Her forefinger poked him in the chest. "What in the Sam Hill do you think you're doing?"

"Damn. I figured you'd take one look and know. You mean, you can't recognize mulch?"

Her eyes narrowed. "Don't mess with me, Mac-Dougal."

He didn't look repentant for teasing her, but he sidetracked to more direct information. "I checked the pH a couple days ago. You're fine there, although you'll probably want to put on some lime in the fall. The mulch was critical, though, Cam. Thursday, we're forecast a major rain. Obviously you wouldn't normally mulch with the plants starting to bud and you still hustling to get the pruning done. But you've got a decent chance at a crop, at least if you can bolster the drainability—"

"*MacDougal.* I know what mulch is. I know what it's for. And I know the damn lavender needs a ton of mulch. But I have no possible way to afford it right now."

"I'm paying for it."

"No, you're not," she said.

"Yeah, I am. Your sister agreed."

Camille pushed a startled hand through her hair. "Violet agreed to let you pay for this?"

"She agreed to let me temporarily help you two out of a mess. You're doing the lion's share of the work. But obviously there are a couple things you can't do totally on your own." He scratched his chin. "I'm having a case of déjà vu. Didn't we already have this exact fight before?"

He was having fun. Too much fun, she decided. "I'm going to punch your lights out. Do you remember that part of the fight from before?"

"I remember the threat." His eyes glinted at her again. He seemed to remember exactly what he'd done with the threat the last time.

"Pete. You should have told us you were doing this. Not just shown up with strangers."

"Whoa." Pete turned sober, glanced at the workers to make sure the project was progressing, and then steered her deeper into the shadows of the maple. "Cam, I did tell Violet. She knew I was bringing in the mulch. I really wouldn't have just shown up with a crew unannounced—no matter how bossy you think I am. I only moved fast because of the weather. If we really get three or four inches of heavy rain before this is mulched, you could ruin the crop."

"You told Violet," she repeated.

"Yeah. Because we both discussed that Violet needed to be consulted on what her plans were. And her idea was to pay me from the crop profits, so there was no charity involved."

"MacDougal, don't try selling horse spit to a horse owner. My sister doesn't have a clue how she's going to harvest this or what she's going to do with it."

"Yeah, I got that impression, too. She went on and on about how she loved the lavender, but some days, trying to get a commonsense answer out of her is an uphill job."

"Don't you start on my sister!"

"I'm just trying to be straight with you. She's all excited, full of pipe dreams, but I couldn't get a realistic plan out of her—and apparently you couldn't either. The thing is, you're working your tail off, and whether your sister gets a clue about the situation or not, certain things are cut-and-dried. You've got a shot at a crop and some long-term profit—*if* the field's taken care of. So the only thing that makes sense is to bring the field back, help it become all it can be, and then try to get your sister involved in the decision-making process as soon as you can get her a brain transplant. Preferably from a brunette."

She heard him. But it seemed to hit her like a flash of light, that she'd somehow joined life again. They were arguing about a real-life problem. She was participating in the argument. More to the point, all the life around her was seeping into her consciousness.

Clouds were puffing across the morning sky like baby steam engines. She could smell the lazy spring wind, the turned-over dirt. The workers—Pete's employees—were pitchforking mulch in a rhythmic fashion, their laughter and chatter competing with the sound of the tractor blade still pushing mulch. The whole field smelled lushly rich and earthy. And the beautiful lavender…oh, it still looked like hell; Camille wasn't even halfway through the impossible job, and it was ridiculously late in the spring to believe she could make this happen. But the lavender was trying so hard, in spite of its earlier neglect. Every lavender plant showed growth. Green spurts. Buds. Reaching for the sun.

Her gaze wandered back to Pete, and then couldn't seem to let go. This morning he was wearing khakis, work boots, a short-sleeved shirt. His hair kicked up in the breeze. She could see the creases he'd gotten from past summer suns, the frown lines from other life experiences, the laugh lines bracketing his mouth.

She remembered that mouth…remembered it wooing hers, teasing hers, intimately taking hers. She remembered the artwork of hair on his chest, the color more mahogany, more lustrous, than the hair on his head. She remembered his muscled shoulders and tummy, those long, long legs, those funny feet.

"Did you hear me?" Pete demanded.

Really and truly, he had ugly feet. Big. Huge toes.

"I just suggested your sister needed a brain transplant," he said, as if to make certain she'd heard that insult.

She'd heard his teasing the first time. But she remembered those big, ugly toes rubbing against her in the night, remembered folding into his arms, remembered feeling hunger and a fury of passion and how erotically and ardently he'd taken her in. And suddenly fear welled in her throat so thick she could barely swallow. She blurted out, "I can't help it if I still love Robert."

As if he instantly understand her segue to a completely different subject, he said, "Who asked you to help it?"

"You didn't ask. But I'm afraid of hurting you, Pete."

"I'll be damned. For some reason, do you think you're talking to a boy? Because I'm a grown man, and it isn't up to you whether I get hurt or not. It's up to me. And I can handle my own life."

She tried again, struggling to understand the welling fear inside her, to be honest with him. "It's easy for people to tell me to move on. I'd be thrilled to move on. But ever since the trial…it's as if this door were locked and bolted inside me. I can't imagine loving anyone else that way again. It's not that I don't want to. It's that I don't think I could survive losing anyone else, volunteering for that kind of hurt, that kind of risk. I don't think I have that kind of love inside me. Not anymore."

Pete cocked a leg forward. "Did you think someone was asking you for love?"

Her eyes searched his. Actually, she'd thought just

that. That he needed love, that he deserved it, possibly more than any man she'd ever met. That he'd needed something from her, no different than she needed something from him. But now, he sounded so aggravated and huffy that she wasn't sure. "I just…wanted us both to be clear about what was going on."

"Damn good sex is what went on, Cam. The best sex I can remember. Chemistry that was over the top. If you feel differently or are trying to tell me that you regret it—"

"I don't regret it."

"If you want something more from me…"

Sheesh. She could feel the bristles climbing up her spine at his tone of voice. "I don't want a damn thing, you blockheaded dolt! And there's nothing wrong with 'just sex' either! Everything doesn't have to end up in a complicated, heavy relationship, for heaven's sake!"

"So what's the problem?"

"There is no problem! And don't you forget it!" Before he could even try saying anything else, she whipped around and stomped off.

Since it was Campbell lavender his workers were sweating over, she knew she should pitch in and be part of the mulch project. And she would. But just then she needed to dunk her head in a bucket of water to cool off. Try to be nice to the damn man and where did it get her? He didn't want to be cared about. Well, fine.

She didn't want him to care about her, either.

She walked so fast that she got a stitch in her side—except that somehow, that stitch seemed to locate right over her heart, and ached worse than a bee sting.

Eight

The only reason Camille went up to dinner was because she knew Violet would raise hell if she didn't. Still, she went to the trouble of unearthing some blush and lipstick—not for vanity—but hoping some face paint would hide her real mood from her sister.

As she crossed the yard to the farmhouse, though, her heart felt heavier than mud. Man. She thought she'd shaken the worst of the dark funks in the past couple weeks, but the dragon had come back to bite her in the butt since arguing with Pete that morning.

It seemed as if every direction she turned, she was doing something wrong. Darn it, she was still living like a kid on a campout. She still couldn't seem to imagine a regular job, and couldn't dredge any interest in ever going back to the marketing work she'd once loved. She'd gotten herself involved with a man who'd been hurt by a woman before, and so had his boys.

And if she didn't get her head on straighter, she risked
hurting them, too. And she wanted and needed to help
her sister do *something*—the problems with the lavender
field being an obvious way Vi needed help—only Camille couldn't cope with that alone, either.

"Uh-oh," Violet said the minute she walked in the
door. "What's wrong?"

"Nothing! I'm totally fine. Let's talk about you."

But Violet had always been her most annoying sister.
Once Vi got it in her head there was a problem, the
fussing never let up. No matter what she said, Violet
tuned into a pep-up channel. "You're not useless.
Don't be ridiculous. Everybody goes through hard
things. You have to give yourself time to let yourself
heal. Would you go through a surgical operation and
expect to be back at work the next day?"

"Violet, you don't have to be so nice to me. It's
driving me crazy to be such a burden."

"You're not a burden. What you need is strength.
And I made just the foods to help you!"

Violet laid out a feast. Lentil-rice patties. Some kind
of fish with a spinach sauce. Lavender-buttered turnips
and a lemon-lavender loaf. Peachy sweet potatoes.

Camille exchanged glances with Killer, who took
one good sniff and then flopped on the floor with his
eyes closed.

"And I made you a tonic for those headaches you
get," Violet said brightly.

"Thanks so much."

"The sweet potatoes are especially important. They
have a natural estrogen. And the spinach and lentils—
you have to build up some iron, some strength—so I
want you to have double servings."

She glanced desperately at Killer again, but he shot

her a look as if to say: *Don't look at me. She's your family, not mine.*

By the time dinner was over, Camille was hungry enough to chew rope. Not only was the menu inedible, but Violet followed up with a whole bubbly program of ideas—like wanting to give her a massage and relaxation exercises and force her into a warm bath with lavender bath salts. The instant dishes were done, Camille fled with the dog.

She was almost desperate enough to drive into town for some doughnuts and Oreos and other serious staples, but once she got back to the cottage, she changed her mind. Still strewn through the living room were all the packing boxes and cases that she still hadn't tackled. They seemed glaring symbols of how long she'd wallowed in being miserable. She simply *had* to get on the other side of this tragedy. Kick it up. Move on.

So she opened the first box…and immediately found a box of CDs. Robert's CDs. Like the songs he'd played the first time he'd made love to her…and the music he always picked when they were dressing up for a night on the town…and the music he'd played the day they'd painted the kitchen. Her hands jumped back as if burned. She tried to realistically remind herself that she'd never even liked Robert's music—any more than he'd liked hers. But that wasn't the problem. The problem was the singe of memories.

She pushed that box aside and determined, cracked open a giant-sized crate. This one held kitchen supplies—only not the usual array of practical pots and pans—but wedding gifts. Sterling silver cake plates and fondue pots and butter warmers and waffle makers— still as new as the day she'd opened them and warmly promised the gift givers that she'd cherish and use their gift every day of their married lives.

Okay. So that was another throat-tightening box, but stubbornly she reached for a different one. This carton should have been memory-safe, because it held nothing but clothes—winter sweaters, hers, nothing that belonged to Robert. Except that the first item on top was the green sweater he'd bought for her last birthday. She remembered opening it, remembered saying, "Oh, I love it, you darling!" but she also remembered having the traitorous thought that Robert couldn't possibly really know her, because she'd never be able to wear that vomit-green color in a thousand years.

Camille slammed down that box, too, making Killer jump. "We're going to throw all these things out tomorrow," she told the dog. And when Killer didn't look particularly believing, she said, "Come on! I'm not being a coward. It's not like that. For heaven's sake, it's almost eight o'clock and we've been running all day. It's ridiculous to start anything this huge this late at night." But when Killer still looked skeptical, she said a four-letter word and knuckled under.

She couldn't just throw out boxes without looking at the contents, because there were serious belongings in some of them—things she'd need once she got around to putting her life back together. So she sorted, then put box after box in the trunk of her car, then carted two entire trunk loads to the dump. That was all she could possibly handle, though. When she drove back home after the second trek, the sky was midnight-black; the wind had a scissor-sharp chill to it, and she was so whipped that her head was pounding.

She pushed her shoes off at the door, peeled off clothes as she walked, and then simply threw herself into bed. There was no doubt in her mind she'd sleep like the dead.

Or that was the plan.

It didn't seem to quite work out that way.

The dream started with memory flashes from her wedding. Her mom, Margaux, was fluffing her hair, fixing her dress, looking at her with serious-mom eyes. It was her mom who'd waited until they were alone to give her a private present of some lethally sexy French satin lingerie. And her mom who'd said, "You're the most beautiful bride I've ever seen. But if you're not sure, we'll stop this right now, darling."

And then her dad was suddenly in the dream, Colin with his far-seeing blue eyes and the pipe he sneaked away from his wife. To her dad, she'd never been able to do wrong, yet it was her dad who wrapped her in a burly hug and said gruffly, "I never thought a city boy'd make you happy, Cam, not you, but if he's what you want, I'll love him. Just so you know that I'll shoot him if he isn't good to you."

She kept tossing and turning in the dream, because she wanted her dad so badly. She wanted her mom. Just once she wanted to be young again, a girl, safe in her parents' secure arms, Margaux with her wildly emotional nature, and her dad who'd tromp the woods with her, rain or shine. Daisy was suddenly there—Daisy, who was always so exotic and sexy and striking compared to her and Vi. "Don't go to Boston," Daisy said. "He's nice, sweets, but there's just no way he'll hold you for long. Pick a man who opens your world. Don't go to Boston, don't go to Boston."

The dream turned dark so fast. The wedding suddenly became a wild thunderstorm, and the beautiful white dress somehow turned into a devil-black cloud that choked her, pressing tight, smothering he. Suddenly there was an explosion of pain, when a fist slammed into her face. She heard Robert's helpless cry of pain, heard the judge's voice say, "First offense, first offense. Let's not compound this by making more of a tragedy than it already is." She woke up in the hospital, knowing he was dead, knowing her life was over. She heard the scrape of her broken ribs when she tried to move, the fear, the sickening fear of those men in the dark; she could still hear their drug-crazed laughter....

"No, no, no. Cut that out. You're not alone."

Even though it was a dream, she recognized Pete faster than a snap and thought *thank God, thank God*. Like a miracle, he was just suddenly there right when she needed him. Like magic, she could rope her arms around him and be held, as fiercely as she wanted, as strongly as she needed. "I'm so tired of having this stupid damned nightmare," she said.

"Well, you're not going to have it anymore. I'm right here. We're going to chase it away."

A swoosh of a kiss made her head fall back into the pillows. That kiss...it seemed so real. She could taste Pete, smell his night-cool skin, feel the flannel of his shirt, the weight of him in the bed next to her. Somewhere, a window seemed to let in the drift of cool air— real air. Somewhere, Killer grumbled at the intrusion and jumped off the bed—as if the dog had really been snoozing at her feet.

It was amazing, how real some dreams were. Even better, though, was knowing that she could do things, say things, in a dream that she obviously could never do in real life.

"I'm afraid, Pete," she whispered.

"Of course you've been afraid."

"And I just can't seem to stop feeling…guilty. That he died and I didn't. That he tried to fight them off for me, and I couldn't fight them off for him."

"We're not going to talk about him," Pete said, and kissed her again.

Naturally she'd had erotic dreams before—who hadn't? But nothing like this. There was another mysterious dream kiss, than another—each hotter than passion, wetter than a river, kisses that flowed and waved and ebbed all around her. His flannel shirt disappeared faster than a poof, just like magic. She heard some vague shuffling sounds—like his boots dropping—then felt the whoosh of cold night air when the sheets were skimmed off her bare body.

For an instant, she was disorientingly aware that maybe this wasn't a dream, because she really was cold. But then, so swiftly, so easily, she wasn't. Pete's long, strong body covered hers, wrapped her up in his long limbs and warm torso. He showered her with more kisses—kisses like presents, each wrapped differently, each packaged like a surprise. Some were pretty and tender, some soft and bright, some so erotic and exotic they took her breath away.

Some skimmed down her body with his tongue, taking in everything, breast, tummy, navel, thigh, one lick at a time. A night beard teased her tender skin, inflamed her senses. He kept whispering, whispering, "Forget everything, Cam. Just think about this. Just be. Just let me love you."

Something was suspicious.

Mighty suspicious.

Still, she was almost positive the only thing intruding

on this extraordinary dream was her conscience. It was terribly disturbing to realize that she'd never felt this way with Robert. This wicked. This thrilled. As if she could soar, just from the lush sensations of wanting and being wanted, loving and being loved.

Damn it, she'd *loved* Robert, with everything she had, with everything she was. And she was tired to bits of living with that conscience hounding, hounding, hounding her all the time…and tonight, she didn't care what was suspicious or not. Tomorrow she'd try harder to be mean and ornery again, to push people away, to protect herself. But tonight…

Tonight she desperately wanted this dream. She wanted…

Pete.

No one and nothing but him. The lush, wicked sensations of being taken over, taken under. His mouth, teasing hers, taking hers. His hands, moving her to madness, coaxing her to want, to need, to hunger, to feel, to sense, to touch back. To feel alive.

In the velvet shadows, he climbed over her. She felt his thighs, tight, hard, when he coaxed her legs around his waist. He tested her for readiness, found her hot, wet, impatiently more than ready for him, before he plunged in, taking her or maybe her taking him by then—who could possibly tell the difference? They were part of each other, inseparable. Each strained for the next height, climbing together, both furiously wanting by then, not having fun, not anymore. Ecstasy was a serious business. Joy took intense concentration, intense giving.

''Pete, Pete….'' She wasn't sure if she said his name aloud. It seemed as if her heart called him, wooing him, wanting him.

And then they both tipped off the sky, spilled into the universe of each other. One sweet, fierce release followed the next, until she sank into the pillows, into his arms, still panting hard, too spent to talk...but not so tired that she lost the energy to hold and be held. She smiled at him in the darkness, tenderly touched his lips with her finger.

"I didn't know," she whispered. She didn't finish the thought. She wasn't sure there was a finish. It seemed as if everything inside her was a tender beginning, created by Pete, possible because of Pete. She smiled again, nuzzling her lips into his neck, and fell asleep heavier than a brick.

The next thing she knew, sunlight was streaming through the bedroom blinds in ribbons. She felt the warmth on her skin, the sensation of well-being and sleepy security, and lazily opened her eyes. There was Killer, his snout on her sheet, eyes staring hopefully at hers from mere inches away.

"I take it you want to go outside," she murmured.

The dog woofed.

"Exactly when did you start sleeping in my bedroom? The last thing I knew, you worthless mutt, you were sleeping outside."

The dog laved her hand lovingly.

"I'm not keeping you, remember? You don't belong to me. Nothing belongs to me, Killer. So don't get attached."

The dog woofed again, and then reached over to lovingly wash her face. The feel of that long, wet tongue got her out of bed bouncing-fast.

She let the dog outside, then stumbled back into the bedroom and sank on the bed's edge, just for a few moments, struggling to get her emotional bearings. Last night simply had to have been a dream. Really, there wasn't even a question in her mind about that. In real life, she'd never have done those things, felt those things. It was unfair to make herself feel guilty for a dream. It was just disconcerting because everything about their lovemaking had seemed so exquisitely real. The sex was part of that, but the invasive memories that shook her far more were her feelings for Pete, the feelings he'd shown her, how they were together, all the love and tenderness and sensitive caring he'd given her so freely. Obviously, it had been fantasy. A superb fantasy, but nothing she had to worry was conceivably true....

From the corner of her eye, she spotted the sock on the floor. It wasn't remotely unusual to see socks on the floor, of course, and the cottage was an extra disaster this morning because of all her unpacking and box-hauling the night before.

But this particular sock wasn't hers.

This particular sock was as big as a football.

Practically as big as a boat.

Only one person she knew had feet that big—and he was no fantasy.

Suddenly there was no more pretending—especially to herself. Her breath caught, and suddenly Camille couldn't swallow.

She finished an entire row of lavender in record time—and had record blisters to prove it. When she stopped to yank off her gloves, two of the darn blisters broke, and stung like fire.

She hung a swearword on the wind, and then took a long, slow look at the field.

The lavender was barely recognizable from the knobby, weed patch it'd been weeks ago. It wasn't perfect. There was no way to make it perfect in a single year. But the mulch had prettied up the rows, cuddled under the plants, and each trimmed lavender plant now looked evenly rounded, its fronds green and soft. There was no sign of purple yet, but there was a promise of that color, and a hint of the scent in the new growth.

There were still a couple more rows to finish. That was all, but they were *long* rows. Camille sighed. Truth to tell, she'd made two days of headway just this afternoon alone. One advantage to being miserably upset was that she'd worked double fast. The disadvantage was the blisters, the backache and the weak left ankle. She shook her hand, as if wind could somehow chase away the fiery hurt, and then spotted Laurel and Hardy loping over the knoll, in their baggy pants and high-class clippers.

"Hey, Camille." Sean and Simon spoke with one voice and a matched pair of frowns.

"I don't need help today," she said.

"Yeah, well, that's what you always say." Simon ignored her. "Don't start with us. We had a bad day."

She didn't ask. It wasn't her problem, why the boys were grumpy. It was her problem, trying to figure out why the boys' father had climbed in her bedroom window and made love to her until she couldn't see straight.

She had no answer for either question—only four hours worth of blisters to testify that she'd tried her best to figure it out.

Killer, the traitor, hustled from boy to boy to be petted and cosseted, as if the damn dog thought it was loved and desired. Sean always spent some time stroking the dog, but invariably it was Simon who baby-talked and really fussed. Today, though, neither spent much time on Killer. They both worked down a row clip-clip-clipping as if they were both suffering from the same sore tooth.

Camille started on the last row, but without bandages on her blisters, even the smallest clip made her wince.

Sean easily caught up with her, from his side of the far row. "Dad's going to let me get a horse."

"I thought he'd said absolutely no."

"Yeah, well. He changed his mind."

Camille didn't care, but damnation. The last she knew, a horse was the kid's most ardent desire, worth fire and brimstone at the very least. Yet now, Sean couldn't seem to come through with a smile to save his life. "So that's soon?"

"I'm having a little trouble pinning him down. I know I can't even start looking until school's out. But then, I guess. Anyway, she called last night."

The last sentence was tacked on as if it logically followed. Camille sensed that the most intelligent thing she could do was shut up and not invite trouble, but somehow she had to poke out one more question. "Who called?"

"Mom." The tone was disgusted, furious, the head bent way down. "I don't know why Dad didn't pick up the phone. Probably because he doesn't hear it when he buries himself in the study real late. And Gramps—when he's in his room, he can't hear any of the phones anymore."

"No?"

Sean glanced over to where Simon was working. "He talked to her, too. Like we wanted to hear from her, you know? After all this time."

He clipped and pruned, dropping the dead branches in baskets as he went, head still bent as if hiding from a storm.

"It was unbelievable. She leaves us, you know? Because we don't matter enough to her to stay. She doesn't care about us. But now she calls, wanting it to be *okay*. Like sure."

Camille quit pretending to work.

"She says, like, she needed *space*. She says how she felt smothered. She says she was afraid she'd have a complete breakdown if she lived in the country another minute, so that was why she left, because she didn't want us exposed to her going crazy. She didn't want to hurt us. You ever heard such bullshit?"

Simon, who was supposed to be clipping down at the far end of the row, had mysteriously scooched up to the other side of Sean's row. "Don't say bullshit in front of Camille, stupid."

"Why? She doesn't mind. She's like us."

"I don't mind," Camille agreed.

"See. She's no *girl* type. She's like us." *Clip-clip. Clip-clip.* "You know what I told my mom?"

"No. What?"

"It's like she wanted us to tell her it was *okay*. That she just took off on us. Well, it's *not okay*." Sean lifted his face, just for an instant, his eyes aching with fury.

"So we told her just what she'd told us." Simon tucked his head down now. "We told her we needed some *space*. Like how we felt *smothered* living with a mother all the time. So she could just have a real great time with her boyfriend, because we didn't need her. And Dad doesn't need her either, or any other woman, too."

Everybody clipped. A cloud chased across the sun,

than bared it. Sean said, "We were gonna wake Dad and tell him about the call, but we figured he was either working or sleeping, because we didn't hear him behind either door. So we told him this morning."

"He was pretty mad," Simon said.

"Mad at you two?"

Sean and Simon both shrugged. "He said we should have been nicer. He said, no matter what she did, she's still our mother. He said, that the fact of her calling meant that she was at least trying to say she was sorry. I said that was totally stupid."

"I said it was totally stupid, too," Simon affirmed.

"Then he got madder. You think that was fair?"

Camille gulped. "Hey, what are you asking me for? This is between you two and your dad. My opinion isn't worth anything."

"It is to us," Sean said. "We think Dad should have been on our side. And we don't see one single reason why we should have been nicer. Like what kind of excuse is that about needing *space?*"

"It's no excuse at all," Camille agreed.

"You don't leave people you love when it's tough. That's when you stay and stick it out. That's always what Dad said before. Mom just left because she wanted to. Period. She didn't care about us. That's the way it is."

"So why are we supposed to be nice?" Sean demanded.

Both of them looked at her, waiting. Camille threw up her hands. "Look, you guys. I'm the last person in the world you should be asking. I don't claim to have any answers for anyone."

"But that's exactly why we're asking you. You're the only one who isn't always telling us what to do.

All we're asking is what you think, for Pete's sake. Sheesh.''

Sean sounded so disgusted with her that she felt compelled to at least say something. ''Well…what I think…is that it's about time your mom called and started to try to make amends. And personally, I don't see any problem with you being honest with her. You guys have every reason to feel angry. And you have every right to let her know how you feel. It's up to her to figure out what she wants to do about that.''

''See,'' Simon muttered to Sean. ''I told you Camille'd take our side.''

''Wait a minute, wait a minute. Don't be thinking your dad isn't on your side. He just wants you two to take the higher ground. You don't want to do the same thing your mother did, now do you? Run away because something was hard?''

''Hey, we're not running from anything,'' Simon protested.

''It's not like we're afraid to talk to her or anything like that,'' Sean agreed.

''Well, good,'' Camille said. ''Because I think that's probably what your dad's trying to get you to see— that nobody's winning the way it is. Your mom made a big mistake. Nothing she says or does is going to erase that. So maybe you can't forgive her, and maybe you can't accept what she's done, at least right now. But if you can't talk to her—at all—how can it ever get better?''

''What's to get better? We don't need her.''

''We don't need women ever again.'' Simon said. ''Except you. We didn't mean to include you with the creeps, Cam,'' he said warmly.

''Yeah, Cam.'' Sean slapped her companionably on

the back, hard enough to make her rock forward.
"You're one of us. We'd never lump you with the
women. We know we can trust you."

Her heart froze. She'd seen this coming. Pete's boys
liking her, their wanting to depend on her. They *needed*
to depend on someone—a woman—exactly because of
what their mother had done to them. But if she couldn't
get her own life together, what kind of role model
could she possibly be for them?

And if she couldn't be the kind of role model that
they really could trust, she simply had no business em-
broiling her life any closer with Pete and his family.

Nine

The next morning, Camille carted two armfuls of laundry to the house. Unfortunately, Violet caught her scooping up more dirty clothes from the hamper.

"What's this?" Violet said in shock.

"Hey. I've washed clothes a bunch of times since I've been here. Yours, too."

"I know you have. But suddenly you're toting junk to the dump. And you're washing sheets every couple days. And your windows are clean. Could it be… you're starting to feel a little sociable again?"

"Not willingly. More like, I'm working outside so much that everything gets dirty faster."

"Ah. So it isn't about a certain guy half living over at the cottage—"

"Pete is *not* half living over at the cottage."

Violet's eyebrows arched. "Did I say Pete's name? My, we are defensive." A rusted heap of a truck pulled up in the yard. Vi glanced out, and then hustled outside to greet the visitors.

Judging from the conversation, Violet had hired the two men to do some heavy-duty landscaping around the front of the house and Herb Haven.

Camille had just been considering murdering her sister. Man, *no* one could tease more mercilessly than a sister, and Violet was even worse than Daisy. But now, she watched Vi change personalities from a completely normal, pain in the neck sister into Ms. Brainless Ditz again.

It was the men. They were both late-twenties. Sun-bronzed. Their shoulders and arms were ropey with muscles, their jeans riding low, their hair shaggy. Cute enough, but young, and nothing special, really. Just guys.

Yet Violet's whole behavior changed around them. Her laughter came out trilly; her movements mimicked an airhead; she chattered nine for a dozen and acted dense as a thicket.

Camille cocked her hands on her hips, thinking *soon*. She could hardly interfere in someone else's life when her own was still in pieces. But soon, she simply had to figure what the Sam Hill was going on with her sister.

But right then, she scooped up her clean sheets and towels and laundry and hustled back to the cottage. Her goal was to be out in the lavender before lunch. In her mind, she'd set a goal—she was giving herself a maximum of one more week to finish the pruning. Really, it was ridiculously late in the season to be trying to do this kind of work now, but she was close to the end. Once the pruning was done, she'd have essentially done a needed job for her sister—something to earn her keep. What Violet intended to do with the damn stuff from there wasn't her business or her problem.

The lavender was only a symbol, though. Camille knew full well that Pete was welling into a crisis, in both her mind and her heart. But where she didn't seem able to handle Pete, she was determined to handle the things she could. The lavender, for one. For another, she was determined to set the cottage to rights—all things thrown out from her old life, a keeper pile established, the cottage cleaned up for real. And then...

Well, then she needed to make decisions about her life.

She'd been coasting long enough. And if she still wasn't sure where to aim from here, she resolved to stop babying herself.

By the time she reached the cottage porch, her arms ached from the weight of the two laundry baskets. She used her elbow to open the screen door...but then startling her, she heard a mewling sound from somewhere in the living room.

Killer must have heard the same sound, because he immediately initiated a howl worthy of a banshee.

"Shut up, you dolt."

Sometimes he obeyed. This morning, he didn't seem inclined, so she bribed him outside with a dog cookie and closed the door—the fresh air had been welcome on this warm morning, but she couldn't hear herself think with all Killer's howling. And then she turned around to face the towel-draped cage on the floor.

Warily she pulled off the towel, and discovered a mournfully panicked cat. At least, she thought it was a cat. It looked like a pumpkin run over by a tar truck, with a torn ear, a gimpy leg and a face only its mother could have loved.

"Oh, no," she said. "Dream on. This is not happening."

The cat prowled a circle in the cage, mewling pitifully.

"No," she said. "Practice it. Because it's the only word you're going to hear from me." Fuming, she stormed into the kitchen, slammed a bowl on the counter and foraged in the fridge. Almost nothing was in there, no surprise, but there happened to be a couple slices of cheese and the leftovers from a sandwich the day before.

When she came back to the cat, she snarled, "I'll feed you. Because you're obviously hungry. But you're not staying here. I've got one dog I'm not keeping now. There isn't a prayer in the universe that I'll take on a cat, so forget it."

The minute she opened the cage, she assumed the cat would fly out, and either hide or dive for the food. Instead the mangy, hairy thing immediately started up a thunderous purr and tried to climb on her lap, nuzzling her nose into Camille's tummy.

Obviously she had to pet her, but she still put the truth on the line. "I hate cats. Even before, when I was a nice person, cats were just never my thing. That's just the way it is."

The cat, who weighed somewhere around three ton, circled her lap and then settled down, eyes closed, claws kneading Camille's skin through jeans. Probably drawing blood. She showed no signs of getting up. The torn ear looked scabby. It was a monster-sized cat, but Camille could still feel its ribs underneath all that matted long hair. The face looked as if someone had thrown black and orange paint on it in blotches.

"Look. You're not staying on my lap. You're not staying here at all," Camille said irritably.

No response.

"Okay. Look. You can have something to eat and you can nap here for a few minutes. Then that's it. So don't get too settled in."

Still, no response. Camille waited. And waited. But the cat showed no inclination to stop purring, much less to move, so eventually she shifted her onto a chair.

Faster than spit, she grabbed her car keys from the kitchen, jogged outside and snarled, "Killer, come with me." The dog enthusiastically jumped in the front seat and sat down, shooting her a look of complete commiseration. "Yes," she said, "that's exactly what I was thinking. What low-down varmint would do this to me? What pond scum? What worm-brained, conscienceless, stone-headed…"

Cam was still frothing insults when she pulled into Pete's drive. With Killer by her side, she marched to the back door like a soldier on a mission, shoulders arched, spine stiff. She pounded on the back door with a fist, then stepped in and yoo-hooed.

It wasn't as if she didn't know the MacDougal house. The Campbell household had been female to the core, where Pete's family had been testosterone based. The guys likely wouldn't recognize the sound of their own doorbell, so she didn't hesitate to walk in and yoo-hoo. Still, when no one instantly answered, she propped her hands on her hips and looked around.

Nothing much had changed since Pete's mom was alive. Newer appliances, but his mom had always been tuned to a practical channel. The kitchen reflected a floor prepared to cope with mud; the back hall had plenty of stow space for hats and boots; the table was big enough to serve serious-sized platters. Nothing inside had seen wax in a decade. Nothing needed wax. The coffeemaker was a size to give caffeine highs to a platoon, the glasses and silverware sturdy.

It struck her as odd, how she'd always felt more comfortable here than in the house she grew up in—but undoubtedly that was because of the decor, not the company.

When no one answered after a second yoo-hoo, she turned around, thinking she'd search out the bounders in the barns—but then Ian yelled a welcome. Pete's dad caned through the door with a huge wreath of a smile. A gnarled hand scooped around her shoulder and trapped her in a hug. "There now, Camille, I haven't seen you in a blue moon. Got a mug of coffee with your name on it, just isn't poured yet."

"I didn't come for—" She couldn't get that thought out, before both the boys thundered down the stairs.

"Camille! Hey! You never came to visit us before!"

"I didn't exactly come to visit—"

She just couldn't get a word in. First Sean pounded her on the back, then Simon. Ian took off with her sweater. A box of doughnuts was shoved in front of her—well, part of a box, anyway. There seemed to be two left, not looking too scarily stale. Coffee splashed over the side of the mug. Ian's sneaky grin reminded her of his son's—too much so.

"We don't fuss much in this house. Paper towels do as well as napkins, you know? But you never were the kind to care about those kinds of things—"

"Well, no, of course not."

"We told you, Gramps. She isn't like a regular woman."

Camille touched her forehead, thinking that if she

heard that one more time, even one more small time, she might just shriek. Exactly. Like. A. Regular. Woman. "Mr. MacDougal, I'm really glad to see you, but honestly, all of you, I only came about the cat."

"Cat? What cat?"

Sean said swiftly, innocently, "Dang. I wonder where Dad is."

"Gramps, you should see what she did with Darby. He's like this sweet old thing now—"

"The cat," Camille repeated firmly.

Both boys stole another look at each other. "Yup, we're gonna get Dad right away. Gramps, you talk to Cam, okay? Like make her have another doughnut, okay? Okay?"

"Okay," Ian said peaceably, and smiled across the counter at Camille as if he'd been waiting years for her to finally visit. "I remember you from when you were knee-high, Pete carrying you on his shoulders, walking to the bus stop."

"Yeah?" She heard a door open, Pete's voice, the door closed, then the muffled sound of two cracked adolescent voices talking double time. "The boys got me the cat, didn't they?"

"Sean? Simon?" Ian's jaw dropped as if such an idea shocked him speechless. "They're sure taken with you," he said, as if the complete change of subject worked well for him.

"Mr. MacDougal," Camille said warily, but he interrupted.

"Just call me Ian. You're practically family."

She intended to answer that, but her heart suddenly started thudding with such alarm that she could barely swallow. Family? *Family?* What in God's name had the boys been telling their grandfather? What had Pete?

And then there was Pete loping toward her from the back study, flanked by his sidekicks. All three of them were wearing flannel shirts, holey jeans, and no shoes. Their feet—my God, apparently that size feet ran in the family. But never mind that; she could feel her pulse zooming off the chart just from seeing him again. It was enough to scare the life out of her.

"MacDougal," she roared, "I am not keeping that cat!"

"What cat?" he asked amiably.

"You know what cat. *No* one else in the county would have done that to me but you—"

"Um, wait a sec, Camille," Simon said honestly, "The truth is—I would have."

"The truth is, I would have, too." Sean added hastily, "I didn't. And Simon didn't. And Gramps didn't. And Dad didn't. But in principle, we would have, because we know you're one of the few women on the planet who could actually love an animal the way we do. But the thing is, we just have so many animals around here that we can't adopt any more strays."

"Our dad would kill us," Simon explained.

"Especially since he finally agreed to the horse."

Pete lifted his eyes to the ceiling. "I did not exactly agree to the horse."

"Yes, you did, Dad," Both boys insisted, and their grandfather immediately took their side by saying, "Peter, I'm quite certain I heard you agree, myself."

Pete shook a finger at each of them, then wrapped his arm around Camille's shoulder and steered toward the door. "We're leaving to discuss this so-called cat in some privacy."

"That's good, Dad!"

"Yeah, that's real good, Dad!"

"You go, Cam!"

There was more of the same refrain, but once Pete closed the door, neither of them had to hear it. "I suggest," he said, "that we drive somewhere totally away from the hearing range of my back door."

"You've got that right. In fact, I suggest we go straight to my place so you can pick up the damn cat."

"That makes sense," Pete said.

He didn't, of course, mean it. He managed to finagle the keys to Camille's car, but only because she blindly assumed he was one of the guys who *had* to drive. Which was true, but in this case, his male thing about driving had nothing to do with it. He needed her to go along, and she did that because she assumed they were driving to her cottage.

They weren't. But his mind galloped around a mental racetrack, a thousand miles an hour, figuring out what to do from here. To get her away from the boys and his father—that was a given. But what to do with her then was a complete unknown.

He turned the key on her car and heard the engine hesitate. He had to bite back a comment about her needing new tires and a tune-up. Only the man in her life had a right to nag her that way. To yell at her about stuff like that. To watch over her.

And that sure as hell wasn't him.

She suddenly turned to look at him. "Pete, you passed right by the road to the cottage."

"I know. I figured we'd go somewhere quiet for a few minutes. Not for long—but I'd like to talk to you where no one's likely to interrupt us, and that includes both my family and yours."

"Oh, well...." She looked as if she considered objecting, but then changed her mind.

That didn't surprise him. There was *showdown* written all over her. Her eyes were snapping fire. Her jeans were as threadbare as everything else she wore, but there was attitude in her hips—pure female attitude, and she was tossing her hair every step—until she got in the car, when she folded her arms in that make-my-day-mess-with-me posture she could get.

He knew—he'd always known—that they couldn't continue on the track they were on for long. Being a climb-in-her-bedroom-at-night-lover had been a lot of fun the first time. And the second. But a romantic impulse was one thing, and not being straight about something important was another. Subterfuge wouldn't work in his life. She couldn't tolerate it in hers. And he'd known a showdown moment was coming. He just wasn't prepared for it at this precise instant.

He drove the back farm road that skirted the acres of the lavender, then farther back, past his McIntosh and Red Delicious orchards, then back to the far nestle of woods.

Several acres of old, virgin hardwoods scattered across a high knoll, then gently sloped down to a spring-fed pond. The MacDougal boys and Campbell girls used to sled that hill every year when they were growing up, the girls trying every girl flirting trick they knew to get the boys to carry their sleds uphill again. The tricks usually worked.

A smile whisked across her face. Although God knows she didn't know it—or admit it—she was getting those unshakably sexy smiles of hers back.

"Yeah," Pete murmured, as he braked and climbed out of her car. "I remember a dozen winters from when we were kids. Just this spot. In fact, I specifically re-member Daisy begging my oldest brother to pull her toboggan. He couldn't say no to her and breathe. Heck, he couldn't say yes to her without stuttering and turn-ing red as a brick.''

"Daisy could make any boy stutter. And oh, brother, I loved all those winters. I was the young one, tagging after all of you older kids, but I loved every minute. Skating on the pond. Sledding that hill." For an instant she seemed to forget how mad she was, because she ambled next to him, looping her hands in her back jeans pockets. "You haven't mentioned your brothers in a while."

He wanted to mention that her asking such a ques-tion was a sign that she was seriously ready to join real life again. Weeks ago, she wouldn't have given a thought to his brothers—or anyone else. It was all she could do to get up in the morning. Unfortunately, now that she was better, she seemed unquestionably in a fast hurry to throw him out of her life. And he was bracing for that—he'd expected that point to come for weeks. But temporarily, he hoped some general conversation would ratchet down the tension between them.

"Both my brothers are doing great. Webster's stand-ing in front of a classroom at Stanford. He's married, got two kids and a station wagon kind of life. I don't think his feet have seen mud since he left the farm. Griff's just the opposite—he's in North Dakota. Mar-ried a woman with a big ranch in her family. He seems to love the life and the work—and the two of them seem to attract kids like mosquitoes. Last count, they had four of their own and another three that seem to be just living with them."

In spite of feeling like an axe was about to fall on

his head, Pete almost started to relax. Both of them instinctively seemed to follow the trail down to the water, Cam so easily hiking next to him. No matter how hard she was trying, it just wasn't an easy morning to stay mad. The temperature had already kicked up in the past hour. A warm breeze fluttered the leaves, allowing sunshine to shiver through the forest canopy in yellow polka dots. A rabbit scrambled across their path. The air was soft, tender with spring smells, and the farm pond was just below them, a diamond, with a whisper of morning mist still dawdling on the far side.

In a curve in the path, they startled a doe and her young fawn, who froze at the unexpected intruders. He glanced at Camille. It hurt his heart, how easily he could share a smile with her, share the magic morning. She belonged on this land no different than he did.

He'd fooled himself into believing she belonged with him. No one to blame for that, of course, but himself.

The mama deer finally freaked and bounded off, her fawn gamboling right behind her, breaking that moment of magic silence...but at least Camille was still talking to him.

"When I was growing up, I assumed all three of you MacDougals would end up back on the farm—same as I thought my sisters and I would never grow up and move off. This was home. I couldn't imagine being anywhere else when I was little. But...you're the only one of your brothers who actually did it, came back to the land," she said.

"Actually, I was the only one who could come back, right at the time my dad needed help. Maybe I would have ended up back here sooner or later, anyway. I never wanted to farm the same way my dad did, but I always felt a draw to the land. I like the heritage and history. Can't imagine working at something where I couldn't sometimes get my hands dirty.''

"Neither of your brothers felt that way?''

"Not that they ever said. There are plenty of acres here. We could have found room for all of us. Maybe they didn't care…but I think, more than that, most men just plain tend to settle where their women are. It seems to be one of those universals. Men wander around, unsettled and uncommitted, until they meet a certain woman. Web and Griff took up new roots from the day they got married.''

He knew the instant he used the word "marriage'' that he'd royally screwed up. She stiffened up like a poker, fastened on a glower, and that was it for the peaceful conversation. "Damn it, Pete. I don't want that damn cat!''

"No?''

"*No*. I don't want a cat. I don't want a dog. I don't want your kids thinking that we—''

He cut in quietly. "Yeah. I know. They were trying to matchmake.'' He thought being honest would help, but she looked even more frantic. So he tried to explain further. "Sean—like you would expect—is the one who brought home the cat. He brings home anything that's still breathing. He knew I wouldn't let him keep it—but he and his brother started talking about giving it to you.''

"You could have easily said *No. Don't do that to Camille.*''

"Yeah, I could have. But the fact is, I thought it was a great idea.''

"How amazing. Why did you think that giving me a forsaken mangy cat was a great idea?''

He ignored that question temporarily and went back

to the point. ''The boys have talked more and more about the two of us getting together, being together. So has my dad. They think the sun rises and sets on your shadow—which is great, but I just couldn't believe it when they first started with the matchmaking talk. As far as I can tell, you're the only woman they trust—or have come close to trusting—since their mother took off.''

''But that's crazy, Pete. I haven't done anything to make them like me. Or trust me.''

He rolled his eyes to the sky. ''I'm not sure you'd see good in yourself if someone slapped you in the face with it. And hell, Cam. That follows through with everything else as well. You can't think of a single reason why I've been sleeping with you either, right?''

She edged back a step. ''Of course I can,'' she said testily. ''Sex.''

''Camille.'' He lowered his voice a full octave. ''You're coming close to pissing me off. And you don't want to do that.''

''I'm ticking *you* off! Try and get this through your head, MacDougal. *I'm* the one who's mad. You leave me this aggressive, killer dog that acts as if he'll attack anyone who looks at him sideways. Then you leave me a cat that looks so bad its own mother would disown it. Like you think I need trouble, is that it? You really think I need more problems in my life?''

He warned himself that she looked ready to bolt and he needed to keep his cool. But just possibly, he was as ready for a showdown as she was, because he leaned over her, glowering as damn hard as she was. ''I think you've done enough feeling sorry for yourself.''

''*What?*''

''You heard me. I think it's time you kicked yourself

in the keester and figured it out. You've been through hell, but you made it through to the other side. You don't need more coddling.''

"Since when—'' her finger started poking his chest, hard ''—did you *ever* coddle me?''

"Since never. Because everyone else was doing it. And if all that coddling had helped you, it'd be fine. But it didn't. In fact, it was turning you into a liar.''

"Liar?'' Her finger poked him again. A totally enraged finger. "I never lie. I'm the most honest person you'll know or ever know, MacDougal.''

"Horse hockey. When you first came home, you were beat up. You were like the lavender, full of weeds and tangles and too choked up to breathe…and way too scared to care about anything. I get it, Cam. I've been hurt. But these last weeks, it's not that way…''

"Oh? You think you're going to tell me what *I* feel?''

"Nope. But I'll tell you what you've been doing. Lying. Making out like you don't care—about anything or anyone. You're nuts for that dog.''

"I am *not!*''

"And you're going to be just as nuts for that derelict cat. You always did have a gift for animals, used to be able to talk down a scared cat or an injured dog, even when you were a scrawny little kid. Maybe you forgot that, but I didn't. You've got to have something to love or you go nuts.''

"In your dreams, MacDougal. I'm not going to be nuts for that cat! Ever! I'm giving the dog away as soon as I find a home for it. And the same thing with the cat.''

"And cows fly. Furthermore, you're totally nuts for my sons. You love them both. So why the hell can't you just say so? What, do you think God'll reach down and slug you if you admit to caring about things again?''

''I don't care!''

''And you don't feel anything. For anything or anyone, right?''

''Right. Exactly right!''

Aw, hell. Arguing with her was a complete waste of time. He didn't know he was going to do it—he swore to himself!—but somehow he was hard as rock; somehow he was fighting this impossible, powerful urge to kiss her; and somehow he knew he was going to give into that temptation unless something drastic happened, fast.

So just as her forefinger was aiming to poke his chest again, he clamped both hands on her waist and lifted her in the air. She shrieked before her sandals even left the ground.

She was still shrieking when he turned her in a circle—she was light, but not so light he didn't need to build up a little momentum—and then hurled her into the pond.

He knew the pond well. Off the shore edge, it went straight down for about five feet. It was a fantastic pond for swimming on a broiling day, because it was spring fed—which meant it was fifty-five degrees. Cold enough to make her nipples pucker, for damn sure. And thinking about her nipples puckering was enough to make his tighten like buttons.

She came up sputtering, and oh, man, was she mad. So, so mad.

He was in awe of the sequence of words she strung together. The only other person he knew who could get that eloquent with swearwords in a high temper was him. The amazing part, though, was watching all that passion and fire pouring from a woman who thought she didn't feel a damn thing.

Before Pete could think twice, he heeled off his boots and dove straight in after her. The shock of icy water slapped every nerve awake. He came up two feet from her, gasping and sputtering. The cold water should have taken care of his arousal. Heaven knew why it didn't.

He'd barely hauled in a lungful of air before he felt a punch of water splashed in his face. Cam splashed him a second time, then in one long stroke swam closer with the clear intention of drowning him—or at least dunking him good.

He deserved it, he knew. And normally he wouldn't mind being emergolated—not by Camille—but just then, there was so much more at stake than her momentary temper. So when she clutched her hands on his shoulders, trying to push him down, he kicked them both several feet toward shore toward shallower water. The instant he could stand, he dragged her wet body against his.

She was right in the middle of reaming him out a new litany of insults when he plastered a kiss on her mouth. The kiss was so wet and hot that it made steam shoot up his veins, where seconds before he'd been shiver-cold. So had she. But she warmed up damn fast, too. When he got around to it, he tore his mouth free.

"Show me," he said roughly. "Show me again how you don't feel. How you don't give a damn."

He kissed her again. Again. He used his body to brace her, to walk her out of the water, climbing to the tall prickly grasses on the shore. Their clothes stuck to them like soggy glue, miserably cold, and still he kissed her. Still she kissed him back.

Out of nowhere, both of them paused—both heaving from lack of breath—and when they tried to gulp in a fresh batch, her eyes opened. Her gaze lost that sexy, foggy haze and suddenly sharpened as if she remembered how mad she was. Her fist came swooping toward his ears, so obviously, he had to kiss her again. Had to peel off her clothes. Had to peel off his.

Sunlight poured down on them as they sank down. The grasses were rough, tingly against bare flesh, and still both of them came together in a frenzy, rolling next to the pond edge, rolling away, the sun blinding him, then her, and always, nothing mattering more than claiming the next kiss, reaching the next level of hunger, inspiring the next touch.

It had never been like this for him. Not even close. His world centered around her taste, her kiss, her touch. For him, she was champagne and velvet, moon and sunshine both. She brought him light. She matched him, passion for passion, touch for touch, stroking him as intimately as he stroked her, braving ways to tease him, to take, as he braved ways to fuel sensations and needs in her.

"So you feel nothing, Cam? No cold, no heat. Especially you don't feel anything for me, right? Beyond a little sexual urge. You don't want anything to do with real life, right?"

"MacDougal?" She lifted up, her hands splayed in his hair, her eyes as fierce as black satin.

"What?"

"I've taken all the grief I'm going to take from you. Now shut up and kiss me."

Sheesh. She was so impatient.

So was he. All right, maybe he was a little rough, but he could feel the desperation building inside of him. Not just the desperate need to have her, but the desperate instinct that he'd never have another chance. He knew she was healing. He knew she was growing stronger, physically and emotionally, becoming more like herself. She was only a blink away from not needing help anymore.

Not needing him.

And that was exactly what he wanted, Pete told himself fiercely. He'd never counted on more.

Never.

This was all there was. These moments, with her thick wet hair, tangling around his fingers, her soft luscious mouth feeding off his. Her naked body slipped and slid against his, her breasts so sweet to the touch, sweeter yet to the taste. Her slim legs were made to wrap around him, her hips made to tighten and take him in. When he first plunged inside her, she let out a soft, hoarse cry that echoed on the spring wind, carried into the canopy of leaves, rustled with longing and need.

''Oh, Pete,'' she said, as he drove deep and hard…and then did his damnedest to drive deeper and harder.

He wanted to love her better than her husband ever had. He wanted her to remember a man who'd loved her beyond all reason, all sense, on a sunlit morning in the meadow by the pool, brazen with love, inspired by how much he wanted to give her, to show her, to be for her.

He understood she was going to always remember the man who died for her. But he wanted her to know irrevocably that there was a man who wanted to live for loving her, too.

Because her back had to be scratched up from the grasses and rough ground, he swung her on top of him, and gave her the power and the reins. There was a moment, in all that fierce coupling, all those sweaty limbs and teeth and hot wet kisses, when she lifted her head with a glorious smile for him. And just shook her head to the sun and let out a wild, joyful, sweet laugh.

But then she swooped right back down to him with a wicked glint in her eyes, and that was the end of the smiling. She took him ferociously, riding him as if she were determined to show this stallion what-for…for damn sure she was going to show this man what a woman could do when she was in the mood.

Needs sharpened, cried between them. Her need was his, no different than his need belonged to her. Hands clasped, lips glued, hips pumped to the same erotic rhythm. She crashed first, one spasm of pleasure cascading into another until she cried out, high and spent. Then it was his turn.

His eyelids closed in release, just needing to breathe for a minute. His arms folded tenderly, tightly around her. He didn't want to let her go. Ever. Didn't know how he could. Ever.

But of course, that was passion and love talking.

Not reality.

Pete really knew this was their last time—and knew that he had to face that. There was no other choice.

So he took this moment…and held on for as long as he could.

Ten

It was over a week later that Camille awakened at daybreak with her heart pounding and her palms damp. Swiftly she climbed out of bed and headed into the kitchen.

The night before she'd left doors and windows open. For the second week in June, it was unreasonably, unfairly hot and humid.

As she fussed around the kitchen, she thought it was edgy weather. Stormy weather. Something-had-to-happen weather…and then almost jumped out of her skin when a gust of wind scraped a twig against the screened door.

She admitted to being nervous. Not because of the looming storm, but because of Pete.

With a mug of coffee in one hand, she started two pounds of ground round sizzling in a frying pan. She forked it around, breaking up the clumps. Her heart felt squeezed-tight and achy, as if it were beating under pressure. Building pressure. She simply couldn't shake the panicked nerves.

It wasn't as if she hadn't seen Pete every single day in the past week. She had. But the boys were out of school now, and they'd been with him on every occasion. All three had pitched in to help her finish pruning and grooming the lavender. Pete hadn't spoken about that wild morning at his pond. Neither had she, because there hadn't been a chance—she kept telling herself.

Down deep, she knew perfectly well that if you sat on a train track and refused to budge, sooner or later there was going to be a train wreck.

Irritably she pushed her bangs off her forehead and reached for a spatula. "It's done, but it has to cool for a couple minutes," she said aloud, but when she turned around, no one was in sight, much less listening to her.

Granted, it was still the crack of dawn, but she still expected the smell of hamburger would at least waken Miss Priss. She scooped a huge portion into Killer's bowl, a smaller version into the cat's.

Like any sane person, she'd tried buying cat food, but Miss Hoity-toity Priss had turned up her nose at every brand she'd brought home, no matter how expensive. And obviously she couldn't feed the derelict, no-account cat ground round and then try to give Killer ordinary dog food, so she was stuck cooking for both of them. If anyone found out she was cooking hamburger for the animals, she'd have to kill them, but really, what else was she supposed to do? Not care? Neglect them after all they'd been through?

"Breakfast," she called out. No one answered. No bodies showed up in the doorway. The cottage was as quiet as a manless house. Peaceful. Still.

Lonely. She tromped around barefoot, searching in the usual sleeping spots. It wasn't as if there were a thousand places to hide in the cottage. She found both of them, snoozing side by side on her bed. Again.

"You *know* you're not supposed to be there," Camille said irritably, and sank down between them. Although Miss Priss couldn't be bothered to open her eyes, she immediately started purring. Damn cat purred every time she was stroked. She still looked like a pumpkin run over by a tar truck, but now she looked like a big, fluffy, well-brushed run-over pumpkin.

When Camille tried to stop petting her, those gold eyes opened and a small wet nose nuzzled into her palm again. Killer, finally realizing someone was getting attention—and it wasn't him—rolled over and moaned. He expected his stomach rubbed, and he'd just moan and whine until he got his way.

So Camille rubbed and stroked, trying not to think about Pete, trying to just concentrate on the cat's soft fur and the dog's thumping happy tail…but then she caught a glimpse of herself in the old, wavy mirror over the bureau.

The damn cat looked as if she should be prancing in a cat show. The dog looked just as well tended. The only appalling reflection in the mirror was hers. Her chopped off hair had grown exuberantly for two months into a downright thatch; she'd slept in an old threadbare T-shirt; her nails hadn't seen an emery board in weeks. She looked distinctly like a woman who didn't give a damn about her appearance.

And of course, she hadn't, weeks ago.

Pete's words from that wild morning kept coming back to haunt her. *Show me. Show me how much you don't feel.*

And for all these months, she'd honestly believed that she was dead emotionally. That she couldn't feel again. That she'd somehow be disloyal if she felt something strong for anyone besides Robert. And all those worrisome beliefs had become painfully bigger since Pete, because she *did* feel things with him. Things she'd never felt with Robert. Things she'd never dreamed a woman could feel—that she could feel.

But now she took one last look at the mirror and jerked off the bed, away from that image. Killer and Miss Priss perked up, looking at her with alarm now.

"Breakfast is already in the kitchen, all cooled down. Killer, you know how to push open the screen door, and Miss Priss, you know where the litter box is. Quit giving me those guilty looks. Everything isn't about you two. I have to be gone a few hours, that's all."

She pulled on clothes, grabbed a purse, and then hightailed it out to the car. Unfortunately, because she'd charged off so fast and impulsively, she reached town before businesses opened. Maybe that was just as well, because it gave her a few minutes to plot and plan.

At nine on the button, though, lights punched on and locks clicked open. By then Camille was primed. She hit a styling salon first, unsure if they'd take her without an appointment, but both stylists took one look and dragged her in. New Englanders, being practical by nature, tended to take people as they were. They regarded her as someone in desperate need of a massive overhaul.

Two hours later she left that shop, and started for the clothing stores and boutiques with her credit card in hand. By then, her heart was thumping like an alarm clock under water, a loud thud thud thud that she couldn't ignore. She was well aware she didn't have an immediate way to pay for all this—except with savings she could ill afford, while she was still out of work. But sometimes a woman had to invest in her future.

She'd failed to do that before, she realized.

She had one more stop to make before driving to Pete's house, and it was something that had to be well thought out and couldn't be rushed. Then, all her clothes and purchases had to be stashed in the trunk to make room for the ninety-pound present parked in the back seat. It wasn't a present she would have chosen for just anyone. In fact, it wasn't a present she'd normally give to her worst enemy. But these were unique circumstances.

As she drove the final mile to Pete's house, she had to swallow every few seconds because her throat kept drying up. It wasn't that easy to build up her courage. She kept thinking of all the messages he'd given her that she'd been too self-centered to hear. He thought she'd only wanted him for sex. He had no idea how much she valued him—no idea what she felt for him at all.

Now—when it was obvious, and could be too late—she realized that's what a man *would* think whose ex-wife had cheated on him.

It's not that she'd only cared about herself. From the start, she'd worried herself sick about his sons—especially that they were having a hard time trusting a woman because of their mother's behavior. But somehow she'd failed to include Pete in that worry. He was so damned strong that it was hard to think of him as vulnerable, but he was the one who assumed a woman would walk on him, not be there for him. Not stay.

When she pulled into his driveway, she'd gotten over the first case of hiccups, but there was no one in sight. Naturally, fresh after lunch, everyone was likely to be outside doing something. Since the far barn doors were gaping open, she suspected at least someone was close by.

Hopefully, Pete. *Please, let it be Pete and let it not be too late.*

She climbed out of the car and then slowly, carefully opened up the back door. The bloodhound stretched out took almost the entire back seat. She was young. Barely two years. And although she opened her sad, mournful eyes when Camille bent down in front of her, she showed no inclination to budge.

"Hey, Camille!" Simon, loping out of the far barn, suddenly spotted her and came galloping over. Then stopped dead. "Oh, my God. Oh, my God. What *happened* to you?"

"Um…"

Simon had always been the more sensitive twin. Immediately he looked stricken that he might have hurt her feelings. "Look, Cam. Don't be feeling bad. It'll grow. You won't always look like this. It'll be okay." Tentatively he patted her on the back. "Really, I know how you feel. That first haircut Dad makes us get before going back to school—it's always a killer. You feel like a complete dork. Not that you look like a dork," he said swiftly, reassuringly. "I'm just saying— I can still tell that it's really you."

"Um…"

"And look. Just because you look like a woman and all…that's not the worst thing, you know? I mean, you could have leprosy. You could have mange. Think about it. Looking like a woman isn't the worst thing.''

She touched two fingers to her temples. Possibly this was proof that her transformation had been successful, but conversations like this with the boys still tended to leave her speechless. ''Um—''

Simon suddenly noticed the open car door and chanced to glance in. ''Holy cow. Who's that?''

She took a breath. ''Where's your dad?''

''He and Sean are at this horse place that sells Morgans. They'll be back before dinner. And Gramps is in town, because this is the afternoon he has his blood pressure checked.''

''Okay.'' Sometimes even desperate plans took some rolling readjustments. If she couldn't immediately see Pete, she had to do something. Perhaps she'd start with taking Simon into her confidence a bit. ''This is Hortense, Simon. She's depressed.''

''Yow. I can see that.''

''Well, actually, I think all bloodhounds *look* depressed. But this one really is. She lost her owner about a month ago—Jerry Abrahams, you know, the cop? He adored her. She adored him. And she just can't seem to stop grieving. Can't seem to get her life together. Can't seem to find the get-up-and-go to, um, get out of the back seat.''

''Yeah?'' Simon reached in, and petted the dog's floppy ears. Hortense opened her eyes and let out a gusty, soulful sigh, but didn't move. ''She is so cool.''

''I think your dad needs this dog.''

''Huh?'' Simon's jaw dropped, but then he stood up and looked at her. ''Oh, I get it. Revenge.''

''No, no. I'd never put an innocent animal between me and revenge,'' she assured him. ''This is an honest thing. I was at the vet's a couple days ago to get Miss Priss her shots. That's how I heard about Hortense. But it was late this morning when I called the vet again and was thinking of your dad. The thing is, this dog is running out of chances. She's losing strength, losing heart. Either she finds someone to help her get over her grief, or she just might not make it. And your dad, Simon… Maybe no one in the universe is better at helping someone like that than your dad.''

Simon stuck his hands in his jeans pocket. ''That's a lot of horse manure,'' he said admiringly. ''You're really gonna stick my dad with that dog?''

''I am. With your help. I'd like to get her inside, where it's cool, and get her a bowl of water.''

''Sure.''

She gulped. ''Maybe this was impulsive. But I think it's a good idea. To be honest, I thought it was a great idea. But I'll listen to you, Simon. If you and Sean think I'm out of my mind…''

Simon quickly shook his head. ''No, no. Hey, Cam, I'm totally on your side. So will Sean be. This is the coolest idea on the planet. He's going to love Hortense. And so are we. And we'll all help get her heart back, you know? God. Sean's going to be over the moon. You can't imagine how happy this is going to make him. And Dad…''

''On your dad,'' she interrupted carefully, ''if he has any problem with this, you can tell him to bring me back the dog. In fact, if you wouldn't mind leaving a message for me…tell him I'll be having dinner around seven. He doesn't have to come. But just tell him that I'll set an extra plate if he wants to talk.''

As she drove back home, her heart seemed to be beating harder than a shaky drum, yet she told herself nothing had gone that badly. She hadn't seen Pete directly, but there was no immediate help for that. She'd set some things in motion that had to be. And there was one other good thing, because Simon had been totally disgusted with how she looked. That was a good sign, wasn't it? And if Simon thought she looked bad, Sean would think she looked worse. So that was extra heartening.

Back at the cottage, she put up with Killer and Miss Priss whining about her absence, but after petting them, she immediately headed for the house. Thankfully Violet was knee-deep in customers in the Herb Haven, so there was nothing stopping her from raiding the house. She carted two armloads of goodies back to the cottage. In the kitchen, she started a simmering French stew with a dash of lavender, baby carrots, sauterne and pearl onions. It was a little too early to make a fresh salad, but she put together a chocolate dip with fresh strawberries.

The clock seemed to be ticking so fast. She dragged the table outside, where it'd be cool and shady in the early evening. She whisked on a blue-and-white tablecloth, then two settings of her mother's silverware and her grandmother's silver candlesticks. Last, she added white lilacs, setting them in jars in the kitchen and living room and on the table.

She checked on the food, glanced at the clock, then ran for the bath. Both animals seemed to think she wanted company in the bathroom. They supervised her entire bath, from the face mask to the shaving legs routine. They fled a safe distance during the pedicure and manicure, but homed back in while she was choosing clothes from her shopping expedition. Last came makeup—and there was a time she'd been pretty darn good with face paints.

By then Miss Priss had leaped up on the sink to insure she didn't miss any of the exciting action, whereas Killer had dropped down to all fours and was snoring from boredom.

"He may not come," she told the cat.

Miss Priss batted at the mascara, tipping it off onto the floor.

She picked it up. "I don't know if he'll understand the message, about the dog. She was like me. Grieving so hard that she stopped living, stopped wanting to live. It's Pete who shook me out of that, you know. Not all the people who were so kind. Pete. Who wasn't kind."

Miss Priss found the lip liner, and jumped down from the sink with her prize between her teeth—at least until Camille caught up with her. "No," she said.

Unimpressed, the cat zoomed back on the sink and searched for more things of interest. Such as the blush brush.

"I wasn't coping," she told the cat. "Pete didn't cope for me. He didn't do anything for me. Instead, he pushed me into doing things. And by pushing me, he forced me to see that I was capable of doing things. I get all that now. But you know what I didn't realize?"

Looking straight at her, the cat batted the brush on the floor.

Camille picked it up. "I didn't realize that he was grieving, too. He's hardheaded, just like me. Too stubborn to realize that getting over the hurt his ex-wife dealt him was terribly hard to do. Moving past any hurt that big is hard. But there comes a point where you have to make a choice."

The cat deserted her. Which left Camille completely

alone—except for her reflection in the mirror. The woman staring back at her looked almost—almost—like a Camille. Her legs were bare, shown off by the sassy red sundress. Her lips were glossed with a scarlet shine, her dark hair pulled back with two jet pins. She was slim. Way slimmer than she used to be, but her figure was starting to come back, and the dress accented what she had. Its fabric draped over her body perfectly. It made a woman feel like a woman, look like a woman, move like a woman.

The old Camille wasn't back. She'd never again be the young Camille that she used to be.

She'd grown up since then.

This Camille, though, had more depth. More potential. And more, of course, to risk losing.

Her eyes looked sultry with the hint of shadow and mascara, her lashes as soft as velvet against her cheeks. But there was fear in those eyes. Not fear of losing. Fear that she'd already failed to love Pete the way he needed to be loved. And now it was too late.

Eleven

When Pete finally pulled in the drive, Sean was huddled in the passenger seat of the truck, silent as a stone. His son reminded him of himself in a sulk. He had the same moody eyes, the screw-you posture, the slouchy scowl.

"Come on, Sean. I don't think I'm being unreasonable. I'd rather you worked on the land with me and your brother. You know how much we have to do this summer. But you can work there with the horses for a month. And if you still feel after six weeks that you want a horse, I'll do it."

"Yeah, yeah."

"You're giving me all this attitude and I don't know why. Give me a break. You know how expensive that horse is going to be."

"I know."

"You've loved every animal that was ever born. But

neither of us is familiar with horses. A horse presents a different range of problems.''

''I know that, too.''

''So don't you think it's a fair compromise? Work with the horses, be around them. Get a chance to see if you really like the animal and what it'll take to keep one. Before jumping in.''

''Dad, for cripes sake. Sometimes I get so sick of your being reasonable. Yeah, that's all fair. Yeah, I want to work with them. But I wanted a horse right now, you know? Why can't you just let me sulk in peace for a while?'' Simon hurled out of the truck and slammed the door.

Pete stared after him, shaking his head. Teenagers.

Both boys had been pistols for a week now—and their grandfather had been just as huffy. Pete pocketed the truck key and strode toward the house, knowing full well the reason for their testiness. The family had assumed he'd blown it with Camille. All three of them had actually believed he and Cam were going to tie the knot.

He'd *told* them it was never going to happen. He'd told them from the start; he'd told them last week; he'd told them this week. His dad had adored Camille from the day she was born, and the boys were crazy about her—so they'd only heard what they wanted to hear.

Pete could hardly confess the personal details, but he knew the truth. A man couldn't hold a woman through family or land or money or any other peripherals. There had to be something inside him that made her want to stay. Made her want to love. Made her want to commit. And Pete had already discovered the hard way, when Debbie left, that he'd never had that mysterious *something*.

"Hey, Dad!" Simon suddenly barged out the back door, leaping down the two porch steps, his eyes bright with excitement. Sean, who'd walked into the house with an old man's despair, bounded out right after his brother with the same exuberance.

"What's going on?" Pete asked suspiciously.

"We got something to show you. Hurry up, hurry up—it's in the kitchen."

He followed, expecting anything—God knows the boys had put him through "anything" in the form of surprises before. Still, he could hardly be prepared for the heap taking up a vast amount of space on his kitchen floor.

The dog looked something like a loose puddle of caramel-colored wrinkles—tons of wrinkles. Pete hunkered down, pulled up an eyelid, and then the other. The eyes looked healthy, and the dog blinked, proving it wasn't dead. Beyond a hopeless moan, though, she appeared comatose.

"Who would do this to us?" Pete asked.

Simon chose to answer the questions he wanted to answer. "Her name is Hortense. And she's depressed, because she belonged to a cop and now he died, and so she's grieving. Grieving bad. She needs love, Dad. She needs us. She needs you."

Pete was unimpressed with those answers. "Who would do this to us?" he repeated.

"In fact, she said that Hortense especially needs you, because you're so great at helping somebody get over grief. And she oughta know." Simon added, "I got her to eat some ice cream when I spooned it into her mouth. But then she went back to moaning on the floor again. Can we keep her, Dad? Can we?"

Pete lifted the dog's head, looked into its sappy eyes,

and shook his head again. "Aw, come on, guys. Do you two have any idea how stubborn a hound is?"

"She said…that was the point. That you knew how to deal with extra stubborn critters."

"But this is a bloodhound. You can't tell a bloodhound *anything*."

"Camille—she said you knew about that, too. She said that was why she thought of you, because you were really great with females who wouldn't listen. She's paying us back, isn't she, Dad?" Sean stood up, hooked his thumbs in the back jeans pockets, exactly the way Pete always did.

"Yeah. And payback in a woman is ugly, son."

Simon stepped forward, doing the thumbs thing now, too. "Well, I think we should keep her."

"Who? Camille or the dog?"

The boys exchanged glances. They weren't going to touch that one with an electric prod, but he saw that hopeful glint in both their eyes. "Damn dog is going to eat us out of house and home. And hounds smell unbelievable when they're wet."

"So? So do we." This logic was irrefutable to Sean.

"I gotta tell you two more little things, Dad. Although I guess they could wait—"

"Hold it." When a fourteen-year-old didn't want to tell something, it meant it needed to be told. Yesterday if not sooner. "Spill it," Pete instructed.

"Camille…she said, like, that you could bring the dog back." Simon hustled to get more in. "Like you could bring it around seven. For dinner. But I told her you'd be okay with the dog. Not to worry about it. I mean, you know she can't take in *another* animal. Not this fast. Not when we already pawned off Darby and the cat on her already."

"So I don't have to go over there at seven unless I'm taking the dog back?" Messages relayed from teenagers always needed clarifying.

"Actually, I think she wanted you to come over for dinner to talk. At seven. Dog or no dog. That's how it came across. But…"

"But what?"

"But then there's the other thing," Simon blurted out. "Someone really messed with her."

Pete whipped his head around, no longer playing. "What do you mean, 'messed with her'?"

"You're not even going to recognize her. That's what I mean. That's why I was thinking about not telling you about dinner. Because, like, if you go over there, don't start out telling her she looks horrible. I mean you'll just make her feel bad. Whoever did that to her…well, it's pretty scary. But I don't want Camille to feel bad, you know? I mean, what's the point. Like you always say, judge the person by what they do, not how they look—"

"For God's sake, son, you're starting to scare me."

Simon threw up his hands in a classic male gesture. "*You're* scared. I took one look and hardly recognized her. So just watch it. It's done now. She can't help it, so be nice about it."

It wasn't possible—not from his son's description—to have a clue what Camille might have done to her appearance. Still, Pete didn't even consider stopping over before seven.

In fact, at fifteen minutes to seven, he'd showered and shaved and put on fresh clothes—but he still wasn't sure if he was going over there. The issue was courage. He'd been avoiding her. Not that they hadn't regularly seen each other over the last week; he'd helped her every single day with the lavender. But with the boys out of school, it had been so easy to travel over there as a trio. He hadn't seen her alone once.

Sometimes a guy was strong enough to take a knife in the gut and some days he just couldn't face it.

Still, he climbed in the truck at precisely five minutes to seven. The hound clearly put a line in the sand. And his boys—and their grandfather—weren't about to let him get out of dinner besides. Since they watched him from the window, it wasn't as if he could turn the truck toward Timbuktu. He had to turn toward her place. And since her cottage was essentially next door, he couldn't drag out the ride to any longer than a minute and a half.

When he parked at the cottage, evening sunlight was shivering through the trees in soft yellow patches. Her porch was shady and cool—and damned quiet. The dog and cat were both slumbering on the top step. Neither budged to make room for him to pass, although the cat at least opened her eyes.

"Cam?"

He rapped once on the door, not quite able to see through the screen. But then she opened it. And his heart stopped.

Gone was the waif who'd come home with her heart broken. The woman in the doorway was barefoot, with long sun-kissed legs. She was wearing a scarlet scoop of a dress, held up with a couple of promises—the straps didn't seem more substantial than that—and it sure didn't appear that she was wearing anything underneath. Her shoulders were as bare as her legs, smooth, golden, the simple fabric sculpting the swell of her breasts and curve of her hips.

Weeks ago, she hadn't had that swell, those curves.

Weeks ago, she'd been all bones, all eyes. The darned woman was still all eyes, but now all that ghastly chopped-off hair was wisping around her cheeks. Her lips were red as sin, her posture sassy. She looked… sexy. She looked…splendiferous. She looked like she could make any man drool without half trying, and she'd made *him* drool even when she'd been a waif.

"You're late," she said.

"I know. I'm sorry." He handed her a bottle of wine. The twins and their grandfather had explained that you didn't go to dinner with a woman without wine. They'd moved him to speechlessness—that the boys would conceivably think they could educate him about courtly manners. The same boys who couldn't stand women. The same boys who never wanted a woman in their lives for the rest of their lives. "It's probably the wrong wine," he said.

"There is no wrong wine. Now before you say anything about the bloodhound—"

He loved dogs, all dogs, any dogs. But just then, he probably couldn't tell a poodle from a pony.

The only thing on his mind was her, and his gaze honed on her face as if irrevocably glued there. He just couldn't look away. She'd changed so much—and changed exactly in the ways he'd hoped. She was visibly on the other side of pain now. Healing, if not fully healed. Spirited again. Full of hell again. Ready for life again.

That's what he wanted for her.

"Pete?" She came closer and peered up at him, as if to make sure she'd gotten his attention. "I realize that Hortense was a bit of a surprise."

It was hard to understand why his heart hurt so

much. It was just…when she'd been a waif, she'd needed him. And then by accident he glanced past her. Past the open door, through the kitchen, where her back door opened onto her shady back lawn. He couldn't see that much, but pretty clearly there were candles lit on a table out there. A tablecloth. Fancy silver. He looked at her in confusion.

"What's going on?"

"Dinner. In fact, let's get started, and then I'll explain about the dog." She ushered him through the house, then out to the table, where she motioned to the chair across from her. She poured the wine and started serving, but her vulnerable eyes kept darting to him. Her hands definitely weren't as steady as the sassy dress and makeup implied—and neither was her voice.

"I was walking in the lavender yesterday. It was a real turning point for me. Every time I went out there before, there was a ton of work to do. But not now. Now there's nothing else to do but let it grow. The field's still a long way from perfect, but the mulch, the pruning, brought it back to life. The buds are almost ready to burst. The scent and the color—it's not there yet, but it's so close. My sister's going to have her hands full with the harvest."

He saw the food. The delicate salad. The roast with a scent to die for. And he wanted to gulp down the wine, but at her last comment, he could barely remember how to breathe. "You're not planning on being here for the harvest yourself?"

"No. Really, the lavender is Violet's project. It's not mine to make decisions about. And I think, finally, that it's way past time I started making decisions about my own life again. It took forever, I know. I've been lollygagging here like a bag lady."

"Shut up, Cam. You were never like that."

"Close." Maybe he wasn't eating, but she was shoveling it in. "What I kept thinking, though, while I was walking through the field was how different lavender is than roses. Roses have to be pampered, tended, fed, cared for. All we had to do with the lavender was give it some lousy soil, trim it up, mulch it a little, and it zoomed back from the dead. When it comes down to it, lavender only thrives on tough love. But you know all about that, didn't you, MacDougal?"

This chitchat was real nice, but Pete had had all he could take. "Where exactly do you plan on being after this?" he asked sharply.

She lifted a finger, indicating that she needed a second to finish chewing, then gulped a bit of wine. "With you."

"I beg your pardon?"

She frowned, noticing that he'd barely touched her food. "You don't like my French stew?"

"Yes, yes—"

"Then eat, Pete."

"What did you just say?"

"Oh. About being with you?" Her eyebrows rose impishly. "I thought you guessed my intentions…when I gave you the bloodhound. When I asked you to dinner."

Okay. He figured out the obvious—that he couldn't rush her; she needed to say things in her own way, on her own time. But he couldn't eat, now that she'd brought up leaving. It didn't matter how many times he'd mentally told himself that she'd only come home to heal and would leave after that. There was still a lump in his throat the size of a mountain. So he just folded his arms on the table and tried to listen.

"Of course, I wasn't sure if you'd come for dinner," she said softly, putting down her own fork and knife now. "I know I've come very close to blowing it with you. All this spring, I thought I was the one who had trouble with grief, MacDougal."

"You did."

"Yes. I was grieving. For Robert. And for the injustice of a life lost. I didn't know how to cope…but then you came along, with your bullying and your tough love. Everybody coddled me but you." She cocked her head. "I guess I'm like the lavender, Pete. Pamper me too much and I just get soft. But if you give me a chance to be strong, that's who I am, who I want to be. Strong."

"Could we go back to what you said about being with me—"

"We're getting to that," she assured him, and handed him a buttered roll.

He put it down on his plate.

"You pushed me back into life. But I was selfish. I didn't realize that you were suffering from grief, too. That you had just as big a loss to recover from as I did. But you had to be strong for your boys, strong for your father, so you never had a chance to deal with it."

"I don't have anything to deal with."

"Pete. I'm so sorry she didn't value you. I'm even sorry for her that she was so stupid. I can't imagine a woman in her right mind leaving your bed or your life—not once I knew, for myself, how much love you had in you. She was obviously completely demented."

It took him a second to figure out that "she" was his ex-wife. How the hell she'd gotten into the conversation confounded him. "Um—"

Her voice gathered strength, came out clear and true and sweet. "I loved Robert. You always seemed to accept that, and I'm grateful, because that was a wonderfully good part of my life. But knowing you, Pete, and seeing how you handled a time when I was terrible trouble...how you accepted me when I couldn't even accept myself...that's a deeper kind of love than I ever knew existed. It's the kind of love I want now. It's the kind of love I'm willing to fight for now. And it's the kind of love that I'm strong enough to fight for."

She sprang up and surged over to his side of the table, but then hesitated. Suddenly she didn't seem so sure of her welcome—but that changed. Faster than the speed of sound, he tugged her on his lap and swooped her tight in his arms. She let out a long, achy sigh and nestled there, her arms hooked around his neck, the sunset dabbling jewel colors through the trees on her face. "Are you going to ever get around to kissing me, MacDougal?"

"I'm going to do more than kiss you," he assured her. "But right now, I'm still trying to remember how to breathe. How to believe. Because I wasn't looking to believe in love again, Cam."

"Neither was I, so revenge is sweet. I didn't want to love anyone. Ever again. But you made me, Pete." Since he was being so poke slow, she blessed the touch of her lips against his. Damn, but her big strong Scots neighbor suddenly wasn't so steady. That forehead of his was still furrowed with the shadow of a frown, his eyes still haunted.

"I love you," he said softly, fiercely.

"I know. And I should have figured out how much you cared, from all the ways you showed me. All that yelling at me. And insulting me. And giving me that dadblamed dog—''

''The one you're not going to keep?''

''I'm keeping him. And the cat. And the boys. And your dad. And even Hortense. But most of all, I'm keeping you, MacDougal. Forever.''

She kissed him again...or maybe he was the one who stole that one. Whoever was taking credit, the kiss started out slow and built up momentum. Who would have guessed that tenderness could be flavored with passion, that their pasts opened up everything they wanted for each other's future?

He'd opened up her world, she thought, but she'd do her best to open up his now. The expert in tough love was about to get his comeuppance. A lifetime of the softest love she could possibly share with him.

He broke free for a moment, murmured, ''Camille, I never thought you'd need me. Not once you felt stronger again.''

''I am strong. And I do need you. I'd like to think we need each other.''

''But you loved your city job.''

She touched his cheek, his brow. ''Yeah. I did love it. But people change. I love the land, too. I love your sons. In fact...I'm kind of thinking about running an animal shelter.''

That made him open his eyes. ''You wouldn't do that to me,'' he told her.

''Aw, MacDougal,'' she whispered, ''you have no idea all the terrifying, terrible, wonderful things I hope to do to you.''

But he would, she thought. Because love had given her that kind of extraordinary power and strength. And she had a lifetime to vent it all on Pete.

Epilogue

It used to take time to set up a transatlantic call, but these days Violet just had to dial. Sometimes the connection was a tad fuzzy, but tonight it was perfect.

Unfortunately, it was early in Provence, and Daisy didn't take well to being wakened up at the crack of dawn.

"Darn, I'm sorry. I can never seem to remember how many hours difference it is between here and France. But I just had to call and tell you—they're gone."

"Who's gone?"

"Camille and Pete, of course. You wouldn't believe how gorgeous she looked. And how happy." Violet swung her legs on the desk, beaming herself. "She was so happy she shined like a sun ray."

Daisy sighed right along with her. "Cut it out. You're gonna make me cry. But man…she is so overdue for some happiness after all she's been through. Did they tell you where they're going?"

"No. Darn it. You'd think after all you and I went through, planning Pete being around her, matchmaking the whole thing, that they could at least have said where they were going to elope." Violet sipped at her lavender tea. "On the other hand, she packed three bikinis and not much else."

"Ah," Daisy said, with that perfect French accent of hers. "So we can relax now."

"Yeah. I'm checking on the boys and his dad until they get back. And somehow between the two houses, there seem to be a dozen animals to watch over. And I don't know what I'm going to do with all this lavender—"

"The point, sis, is what we're going to do about *you* now."

"Huh?"

"We've got Camille settled. But now, *chérie*, it's your turn."

Violet blinked. "I don't understand."

"You don't have to understand. You just relax, and let me take charge. But for right now, I'm going back to sleep. It isn't even dawn yet. Love you, Violet. And on Camille—we did good."

"Yup, we did," Violet agreed, before hanging up the phone. Daisy hadn't made a lot of sense, but then none of the Campbell sisters appreciated being wakened from a sound sleep. She'd counted on having a longer conversation with Daisy, but it didn't matter. They'd talk again soon.

*   *   *   *   *

Look for Violet's story, coming soon from
Silhouette Desire

Introducing a brand-new series from

Katherine Garbera

KING OF HEARTS

You're on his hit list.

What do the mob and happily-ever-after have in common? A matchmaking ex-gangster who's been given one last chance to go straight. To get into heaven he must unite couples in love. As he works to earn his angel's wings, find out who his next targets are.

IN BED WITH BEAUTY
(Silhouette Desire #1535)
On sale September 2003

CINDERELLA'S CHRISTMAS AFFAIR
(Silhouette Desire #1546)
On sale November 2003

LET IT RIDE
(Silhouette Desire #1558)
On sale January 2004

Available at your favorite retail outlet.

Your opinion is important to us! Please take a few moments to share your thoughts with us about your experiences with Harlequin and Silhouette books. Your comments will be very useful in ensuring that we deliver books you love to read.
Please take a few minutes to complete the questionnaire, then send it to us at the address below.

Send your completed questionnaires to:
Harlequin/Silhouette Reader Survey, P.O. Box 9046, Buffalo, NY 14269-9046

1. As you may know, there are many different lines under the Harlequin and Silhouette brands. Each of the lines is listed below. Please check the box that most represents your reading habit for each line.

Line	Currently read this line	Do not read this line	Not sure if I read this line
Harlequin American Romance	❏	❏	❏
Harlequin Duets	❏	❏	❏
Harlequin Romance	❏	❏	❏
Harlequin Historicals	❏	❏	❏
Harlequin Superromance	❏	❏	❏
Harlequin Intrigue	❏	❏	❏
Harlequin Presents	❏	❏	❏
Harlequin Temptation	❏	❏	❏
Harlequin Blaze	❏	❏	❏
Silhouette Special Edition	❏	❏	❏
Silhouette Romance	❏	❏	❏
Silhouette Intimate Moments	❏	❏	❏
Silhouette Desire	❏	❏	❏

2. Which of the following best describes why you bought *this book?* One answer only, please.

the picture on the cover	❏	the title	❏
the author	❏	the line is one I read often	❏
part of a miniseries	❏	saw an ad in another book	❏
saw an ad in a magazine/newsletter	❏	a friend told me about it	❏
I borrowed/was given this book	❏	other: _____	❏

3. Where did you buy *this book?* One answer only, please.

at Barnes & Noble	❏	at a grocery store	❏
at Waldenbooks	❏	at a drugstore	❏
at Borders	❏	on eHarlequin.com Web site	❏
at another bookstore	❏	from another Web site	❏
at Wal-Mart	❏	Harlequin/Silhouette Reader	
at Target	❏	Service/through the mail	❏
at Kmart	❏	used books from anywhere	❏
at another department store or mass merchandiser	❏	I borrowed/was given this book	❏

4. On average, how many Harlequin and Silhouette books do you buy at one time?

I buy _____ books at one time	❏
I rarely buy a book	❏

MRQ403SD-1A

5. How many times per month do you shop for any *Harlequin and/or Silhouette* books?
One answer only, please.

1 or more times a week ❑	a few times per year ❑
1 to 3 times per month ❑	less often than once a year ❑
1 to 2 times every 3 months ❑	never ❑

6. When you think of your ideal heroine, which *one* statement describes her the best?
One answer only, please.

She's a woman who is strong-willed ❑	She's a desirable woman ❑
She's a woman who is needed by others ❑	She's a powerful woman ❑
She's a woman who is taken care of ❑	She's a passionate woman ❑
She's an adventurous woman ❑	She's a sensitive woman ❑

7. The following statements describe types or genres of books that you may be
interested in reading. Pick *up to 2 types* of books that you are most interested in.

I like to read about truly romantic relationships ❑
I like to read stories that are sexy romances ❑
I like to read romantic comedies ❑
I like to read a romantic mystery/suspense ❑
I like to read about romantic adventures ❑
I like to read romance stories that involve family ❑
I like to read about a romance in times or places that I have never seen ❑
Other: _____ ❑

*The following questions help us to group your answers with those readers who are
similar to you. Your answers will remain confidential.*

8. Please record your year of birth below.
19 ____

9. What is your marital status?

single ❑   married ❑   common-law ❑   widowed ❑
divorced/separated ❑

10. Do you have children 18 years of age or younger currently living at home?

yes ❑   no ❑

11. Which of the following best describes your employment status?

employed full-time or part-time ❑   homemaker ❑   student ❑
retired ❑   unemployed ❑

12. Do you have access to the Internet from either home or work?

yes ❑   no ❑

13. Have you ever visited eHarlequin.com?

yes ❑   no ❑

14. What state do you live in?

_____

15. Are you a member of Harlequin/Silhouette Reader Service?

yes ❑   Account # _____   no ❑   MRQ403SD-1B

If you enjoyed what you just read,
then we've got an offer you can't resist!

Take 2 bestselling
love stories FREE!
Plus get a FREE surprise gift!

COMING NEXT MONTH

SDCNM1103